ANNIE M P SMITHSON (1873-1948) wa... Irish romantic novelists. Her nineteen books, includi... *a Queen, Her Irish Heritage, The Marriage of Nurse Harding* and *Th... Weldons of Tibradden* were all bestsellers, with their wholesome mix of old-fashioned romance, spirited characters and commonsense philosophy.

She was born in Sandymount, Co Dublin, and reared in the strict Unionist tradition. On completion of her training as a nurse in London and Edinburgh, she returned to Dublin and was posted north as a Queen's Nurse in 1901. Here, for the first time, she experienced the divide between Irish Nationalists and Unionists, and it appalled her. She converted to Catholicism at the age of 34 and was subsequently disowned by most of her family. She immersed herself in the Republican movement — actively canvassing for Sinn Féin in the 1918 General Election, nursing Dubliners during the influenza epidemic of that year, instructing Cumann na mBan on nursing care and tending the wounded of the Civil War in 1922. She was arrested and imprisoned, and threatened to go on hunger-strike unless released.

Forced to resign her commission in the strongly Loyalist Queen's Nurses Committee, she took up private work and tended the poor of Dublin city until she retired in 1942. During her long career, she did much to improve the lot of the nursing profession and championed its cause as Secretary of the Irish Nurses Union.

In later years, she devoted herself to her writing and was an active member of WAAMA, PEN and the Old Dublin Society. Her autobiography, *Myself — and Others,* was completed in 1944, four years before her death at the age of 75.

Her Irish Heritage

By
ANNIE M.P. SMITHSON

THE MERCIER PRESS
CORK AND DUBLIN

THE MERCIER PRESS, 4 Bridge Street, Cork.
24 Lower Abbey Street, Dublin.

First published by The Talbot Press

British Library Cataloguing in Publication Data
Smithson, Annie M.P., *1873 - 1948*
Her Irish Heritage.
I. Title
823'.912 [F]

ISBN 0-85342-865-4

Dedicated to the Memory
of the Men who Died
• Easter, 1916 •

Typeset by Seton Music Graphics Ltd. Bantry.
Printed by Litho Press Co. Midleton

Contents

CHAPTER I

IN SOUTH KENSINGTON

'My dear Clare, your coffee will be quite cold, and the bacon not worth eating. Do come down from the clouds and tell me what you are dreaming about?'

'I am thinking of my Uncle's letter. Oh! Webbie dear! I wonder what they are all like—these strange Irish cousins that I have never seen!'

Mrs Webb drank her coffee and helped herself liberally from the various dishes on the perfectly appointed breakfast-table, before replying. She was middle-aged, stout and portly, and liked the creature comforts of this life.

But Clare Castlemaine's coffee stood untasted before her, and she was reading once more the letter of which she already knew almost every word.

'MY DEAR NIECE — It was with sincere sympathy and sorrow that I received your letter informing me of your changed circumstances. I cannot tell you how more than surprised I was. We all thought your late father to be a prudent as well as an extremely wealthy man, and it seems strange that he should have practically lost all his fortune by such reckless speculation. But still one hears of such cases now and then, and you may be glad that you have at least a little left from the wreck.

But now that you are no longer separated from us by great wealth, I am wondering would you care to come over and make the acquaintance of your mother's people? We are a large family and not well off, but I think we could make you comfortable for a while. Your cousins all join with me in hoping that you will come over and pay us as long a visit as you like. Just let us know and we will be ready to meet you with a real Irish welcome.

I remain, my dear child,

Your affectionate Uncle,

JAMES BLAKE.'

At the foot of the letter, in an unformed girlish hand was scrawled—'P.S. *Do* come, *please,* dear Clare. Your loving cousin, Angel.'

'Which is Angel, I wonder?' Clare said aloud, 'they are such a large family! Webbie, did you ever hear my mother speak much of her people?'

Mrs Webb considered for a moment.

'No, my dear,' she said slowly, 'I don't think she ever referred much to them—at least not since I knew her. You know they never really forgave her for marrying as she did. The Blakes are an old Catholic family, and your poor father being not only English, but a declared Agnostic, was their direct opposite in every way.'

Clare Castlemaine wrinkled up her pretty forehead in perplexity. She could not remember her mother, who had died when she was only a few months old, and hers had been a very lonely childhood, although she was brought up in luxury and had splendid nurseries, expensive toys and clothes of every description, a highly trained head-nurse, with various under-nurses, and in fact all the care and attention with which wealthy people surround their children nowadays. Later on came governesses and masters, and then a finishing school in France. It was strange that the girl was not spoilt, brought up as she had been, for her father idolised her and would never allow her to have a wish unfulfilled, if he could help it. He was a very wealthy stockbroker—a man who seemed to really change everything he touched into gold—his name was one to conjure with in London financial circles, and when he died suddenly from cerebral hæmorrhage, a few weeks before this story opens, and it was discovered that he had been losing heavily and lately had taken to reckless speculation to retrieve his fortunes, with the result that he died almost penniless, the astonishment of all those who knew him was unbounded.

His daughter Clare, who was now twenty-two, had a small annuity of £50 left her by an aunt some years ago—beyond that she had literally nothing. Luckily there were few outstanding debts, and the sale of the furniture and other effects of the house in South Kensington would more than pay all and leave Clare a fair amount of money in hand. Then she had a most exquisite wardrobe of every description of clothes, and her jewellery, so that she was not left so destitute as she imagined. Still for a girl reared as she had been, the change in her fortunes would be very great. Her sole income fifty pounds a year! 'Just about the price of two decent frocks!' she thought with a gasp.

Mrs Webb had been her companion for some years now, she was a very distant connection of her late father's and being left a widow with limited means had been only too pleased to fill her present position. It was now three weeks since the death of Mr Castlemaine, the sale was to take place within the next week, the house given up and the servants discharged. Mrs Webb was returning to her people in the Midlands, and Clare, feeling like a lost child—so helpless and wretched, overwhelmed with her unexpected trouble—had been considering what on earth she could do, or where she could go for a while until she became more used to her altered circumstances. Even in this short time she had discovered that in the eyes of the majority of those who had made up the circle of her friends and acquaintances, she was now a very different person to the rich Miss Castlemaine, who had always been such an honoured individual amongst them. They were civil and friendly more or less but since her position had become known calls and letters of condolence and sympathy had become fewer and colder, and amongst all those whom she had known and entertained so lavishly in the past, not one real friend had come forward with offers of help or hospitality.

James Blake, her mother's brother, had written from Dublin when he saw the notice of her father's death in the papers—a sympathetic, friendly letter. It was the first time that she had held any communication with her Irish relatives, and on the spur of the moment she had replied to his letter and written fully, telling him of her father's financial losses and exactly how she was left. The letter she had received this morning was her uncle's answer, and she was now pondering it all over in her mind and wondering if she should accept the invitation or not. In some ways it seemed the very thing, but somehow she shrank from these unknown relations with their Irish upbringing and environment.

'Oh! Webbie!' she cried, 'what would you advise me to do? Do you think I should go?'

'My dear, you must please yourself,' said her companion, as she placidly spread marmalade on her toast. 'In some ways I think it would be an excellent plan—complete change of air and scene, a new life altogether for you, and in a large household like your uncle's you would be bound to be taken out of yourself and that would be really good for you. But on the other hand I don't know how you would amalgamate with your cousins' ideas and with their mode of life. Still, for a visit—and after all you need not stay unless you care. You know, my dear girl, that my little home, humble as it is, will be always open to you and I don't need to tell you how really welcome you will always be to your poor Webbie.'

Her voice broke as she tried to smile, for she was very fond of Clare Castlemaine, and all this upset and change was a real heartbreak to the good-natured soul.

'Oh! Webbie! I know—I know!' and Clare patted the fat hand near hers. 'You are a dear! But I think I will go over to Ireland for a while—just to see what it is like. They can't eat me, anyway!' trying bravely to laugh, 'but I wish you would tell me all you can remember about my mother for you know Father could never bear to speak about her. Of course I know she was very beautiful from the painting in his study, and I know she was Irish and a Catholic, and that he adored her—and yet, somehow, I always have the impression that my mother was not really happy.'

Mrs Webb considered for a few minutes before replying.

'I only saw your mother a few times altogether,' she said then, and she spoke slowly, as though trying to remember better—'she was very beautiful and very young—not like you in appearance Clare, for although you are very lovely too, you have the fair colouring of your father's people, and your mother was dark, with the most lovely dusky sort of hair and beautiful big grey eyes with such long lashes. She had the sweetest voice and accent I think that I have ever heard, and a lot of little fascinating mannerisms and gesticulations—something like a Frenchwoman, but then the Irish and French are alike in many ways, you know. She adored your father—it was a mutual love and certainly a case of extremes meeting, for two people more unlike in every way I never knew. Yet, as you say, she never seemed really happy—it would be difficult to understand why, for your father grudged her nothing, he surrounded her with every luxury and comfort he could think of—another woman would have been quite spoilt! Of course there was one thing he refused her which I believe she took very much to heart.'

Mrs Webb paused for a moment, but Clare said eagerly, 'Oh! go on Webbie? What was it that my father refused her?'

'Well! it was a question of religion. He refused to allow you to be baptised and you were not to receive any religious instruction. This distressed your mother very much for she was a devout Catholic, and her religion always seemed to be very precious to her, but to all her tears and prayers in that direction your father turned a deaf ear. He allowed your mother full liberty in the matter of her own religion, but you know his ideas about children—to teach them nothing and let them form their own opinions when they are old enough to judge for themselves. I think his refusal to have you baptised really broke your mother's heart—she was never the same afterwards, not that she lived for long, poor thing!'

Clare sighed.

'Poor Mother!' she said softly, 'and poor Daddy, too! Look at the result of his system in me. Here I am at twenty-two years of age, with no religious beliefs at all, quite unable to make up my mind amidst all the various sects I see around me. Why, Webbie! to me it seems impossible to tell which is right, how could I ever decide? You know I have been looking up the subject lately and what do I find? Chaos everywhere! High Church, Low Church, Broad Church—all totally different in belief and practice, and that within the pale of the Established Church alone, without mentioning the hundreds of dissenting sects multiplying every day. The whole thing is too bewildering, and I think Daddy must have been right in his opinions after all.'

'Oh! my dear! don't talk like that! I can never think of you as a woman without a religion—you were not meant for that! If you would only put aside these queer notions and not be worrying over such things, but go to Church—for of course you would never think of joining the dissenters, they are not our class—and say your prayers and behave like the other girls of your age—Oh! how much happier and contented you would be!'

'Now Webbie! have some sense please! This is the age of heredity, and here am I, the offspring of a most extraordinary union; on one side I have as the paternal element a sensible, rather stolid business man, essentially English, with little or no imagination, in fact a materialist in every sense of the word. On the other hand for my mother I had a Catholic Irishwoman, imaginative, religious, sensitive and impulsive—in other words a typical Celt—as great an idealist as my father was a materialist. Now Webbie, if you have ever studied eugenics, what I ask you, solemnly, do you expect me to become, as the result of such a union?'

Then she suddenly laughed as she caught a glimpse of Mrs Webb's bewildered and rather shocked expression.

Clare stooped and kissed her.

'Never mind, old darling,' she said, 'it is all on the Lap of the Gods! Who knows how I may turn out yet? Perhaps I'll enter a convent and live in dungeons behind iron bars and never be allowed to see daylight any more—like that girl we heard about at those "No Popery" lectures you dragged me to once!'

'My dear!' said Mrs Webb, trying to speak sternly, 'You shouldn't laugh at such things, and I only hope and trust that you won't imbibe any of the religious beliefs of your Irish cousins. That would be really terrible.'

'Don't worry dear,' said Clare with a smile, 'I don't think there is much danger in that direction. And now Webbie, come and help me to go through my things until I see what I will take with me to the "little green Isle", and what I will leave in your charge. And then I must write to Uncle James and tell him that I hope to be with him next week—I can settle the day later.'

Now that her mind was really made up, Clare felt brighter and happier in every way. Her father's sudden death had been a great shock to her, although her regard for him was more that of quiet affection than real love, while Mr Castlemaine simply adored his daughter and since the death of his wife had lived only for the sake of the girl. But like all men of his undemonstrative type he had not shown this openly, and perhaps Clare never really knew how dear she had been to him. Once the shock of his death was past there had come the realisation of her changed circumstances and poor Clare felt as if Fate had indeed proved unkind—but she did not want for courage and grit and was determined not to let herself 'go under' in the battle of life if she could possibly help it. According to her present convictions she had only one life to live—one life that she could be sure about anyway—and she meant to try and get the best she could out of it. The girl was a strange mixture—as she had remarked herself, she was the child of a strange union—and had inherited traits from both her parents. So far the parental element had predominated, but this was largely due to environment, and Clare was anxious herself to see if any hidden qualities derived from her Irish mother would show themselves better if she was transplanted to Irish soil. Almost unknown to herself she had always felt a strange wish for Ireland and the Irish, and yet they were a sealed book to her; —like the ordinary English person she knew as little of the real Ireland of today as she did of the North Pole; in fact, she probably knew rather more of the latter spot. But almost unconsciously Ireland was calling to her, the cry of dark Rosaleen was coming across the water to this child of an Irish mother, and she found herself looking forward with strange eagerness to her visit to her mother's country.

She was sitting on the floor of her dressing-room surrounded by frocks and gowns and 'chiffons' of every description, and although she was trying earnestly to help her maid in deciding what to take with her and what to pack away, her mind was full of day-dreams of the future and she found it very hard to attend to the business in hand.

'And after this week I won't have Annette to look after my things—I will have to attend on myself and do my own hair and everything! Oh! I must be sensible and not let my thoughts wander any more,' she sighed, but then suddenly rousing herself she said to the maid: 'We had better go through the contents of this wardrobe first, Annette, and then I can give you all my coloured things to put away and let the trunks be sent on to Mrs Webb's house. There are two black dinner frocks here which I think I will take with me.'

And so with an effort Clare flung herself into the details of her wardrobe and tried to forget for a while her present sorrow and the unknown future.

CHAPTER II

HER MOTHER'S PEOPLE

The Blakes lived in a large old-fashioned house in Rathmines, and on this bright September morning they are gathered round the breakfast table discussing a letter from Clare Castlemaine, the contents of which their father had just made known to them.

'So she will be here in two days. It is well we have a spare room ready. If Molly Dixon had come for her holidays we would have been rather cramped.'

This was from Mary Blake, the eldest girl of the family; she was now twenty-seven and since her mother's death, thirteen years ago, had been her father's right hand—the stay and support of the motherless household. Indeed she was so completely unselfish that she was apt to be put on one side as a matter of course by the younger members of the family; they all loved her of course—it was to Mary they had gone with their childish griefs and tales of woe, and it was to Mary they still went in any doubt or trouble, but the thought that Mary herself would ever need a bit of cheering up or amusement never entered their heads; and this was mostly her own fault, for she had a habit of effacing herself at times, and also the management of her father's large household on their rather limited means absorbed most of her time and attention. But two members of the family valued Mary at her true worth, and those were her father and her brother Tom.

'Of course she will have to be given the best bedroom and the best of everything, but I expect she will not think much of this establishment after her lovely London house. I suppose she will have lovely frocks—what a pity she is in mourning!'

And Nora Blake sighed; she was a pretty piquante little thing of nineteen, the butterfly of the family. She was employed as typist in the office of a large city firm and did her work well, but during her off time and holidays Miss Nora enjoyed life in her own way, and indeed altogether she generally managed to have what she called 'a good time'.

'That's like you, Nora! always thinking of what you will put on!' remarked her brother Pat, a medical student of twenty-three, studying hard for his finals these days and not too sweet-tempered in consequence.

'Of course she will be thoroughly English in every respect,' said Shamus, a tall young fellow of twenty-five, with a very handsome face and splendid grey eyes. 'I don't suppose we will ever make anything of her from an Irish standpoint!' Shamus was a keen Gaelic Leaguer, and cared for little else.

'For Heaven's sake don't start cramming Irish down her throat the minute she arrives!' said his sister Bride.

'And don't you drag her round the slums, and parade her down the Coombe highways and byeways!' was the brotherly retort.

Bride was secretary to an influential philanthropic society, and a great social worker. She lived for her work amongst the poor and existed in a whirl of district visiting, free breakfasts, social clubs and committee meetings.

There were three other members of the family present although they had taken little part in the conversation. First, Mr Blake himself, a thin, grey-haired man of sixty, a solicitor in a fair practice. He was devoted to his children, but the cares and expense of such a family, and the loss of his beloved wife while they were yet so young had lined his face and whitened his hair. Only for his daughter Mary, James Blake often wondered how he could have managed at all. His eldest son, Tom, was seated near him, quiet and intellectual, twenty-nine years of age, the eldest of the family and doing well now as an architect, helping also towards the support of the household—upright, sincere, and good-living, a son any father might be proud to own. Tom was the greatest help to Mary, too, for his words carried authority with the younger ones.

His sister Ursula was seated beside him; she was a very pretty girl of twenty-one, with soft dark hair and grey eyes, very quiet and serious on the surface, but with a fund of hidden fun and gay nonsense that sometimes surprised those of her acquaintance who, previously had only known the serious side to her character. She was to enter the Poor Clare Order as a novice in a few months' time, and at present she was a teacher in a girls' school.

Breakfast was drawing to a close. It was nearly nine o'clock and most of the family had to be at their various occupations before ten o'clock.

Mr Blake rose from the table, gathering his letters and papers together preparatory to setting out for the offices. Clare's letter he handed to Mary.

'You had better keep that, my dear,' he said.

One by one the family gradually dispersed, and Mary Blake was left alone in the shabby and rather untidy breakfast room.

She glanced down at the letter in her hand with a little sigh—it would mean added work and worry for Mary, but as she read it once more a smile broke over her face.

'It's a nice letter!' she said softly, 'and she seems lonely, poor soul! I hope she will be happy with us—we must try to make her feel at home.'

The breakfast-room was in the basement at the back of the house—a long, low-ceilinged room with two windows to the side and glass door opening on to some stone steps which led up to the garden. A fair-sized garden too for a suburban house and well cared for—Shamus Blake saw to that for he was devoted to gardening, and spent a good deal of his spare time, when he was not engaged in work for the Gaelic League, in planting and transplanting, hoeing and digging. Through the day he was hard at work in his father's office for he was destined to succeed to the solicitor's practice, and strange to say, although he was a bit of a poet and an idealist in many ways, still he gave every promise of becoming a clever lawyer.

The kitchen was on the other side of the passage to the breakfast-room, a little further down the corridor, and thither Mary Blake now betook herself.

Sarah, the old servant who had been with them for many years now—since before Mrs Blake's death—looked round as her young mistress entered and her face brightened. She was devoted to all the family, but she adored Miss Mary. The Blakes kept one other servant, a strong young girl who did most of the upstairs' work, answered the door and could wait at table when necessary. Mary had trained Maggie, for she had come to them when very young and ignorant, but was now quite capable; still Mary helped a good deal herself; she was fond of house-work, and also had a special gift for fancy cookery, making the most delightful cakes and puddings easily and with little outlay.

'Sarah,' she said, advancing into the large old-fashioned kitchen, 'Miss Castlemaine will be here on Thursday, so I will want Maggie to help me this morning to clean out the spare room—I want it to be extra nice because you know our new cousin is English, and, no doubt, very particular, for she has been used to a beautiful home in London.'

Sarah stood in her favourite attitude with arms akimbo.

'Do ye tell me that now?' she replied with the outspoken freedom of the Irish retainer. 'Well! Miss Mary dear, if the house that's good enough for the *Blakes* isn't good enough for *any* English lady, no matter had she the wealth of the Ingies itself—well 'twould be a quare thing!'

Sarah had not taken kindly to Clare's advent, but Mary knew the old woman so thoroughly that she could nearly always coax her into a reasonable mood.

She smiled now as she replied.

'Yes, that may be so Sarah, but we want to show this English young lady that we poor Irish can have nice homes and dainty rooms too—so I am going to take Maggie this morning and have a real turn out upstairs. But if you are very busy Sarah and want help, get Mrs Murphy in for the day.'

'Ah! not at all Miss Mary dear!—Not at all! I can manage grand—I'm not that ould and stiff yet, thanks be to God! There's as much work in me ould bones as there is in many a young whipper snapper going the roads these times!'

'All right, Sarah, I'm going up to see Miss Angel—you can send Maggie to me later.'

Leaving the kitchen Mary went up the short flight of stairs to the large hall above, on the right of which was the drawing-room and the dining-room to the left, both large airy rooms. The furniture in each was old-fashioned and a bit shabby, but good still and kept in perfect order by Mary's capable hands. Wide shallow stairs led to the first landing where her father's bedroom was, and also the rooms of two of the boys, her own spare room, and the 'schoolroom'—now used as a kind of general untidy place where the family gathered at odd times and where they could be as noisy and as free and easy as they liked. The landing above contained the girls' bedrooms, and above that again were smaller rooms where the servants slept and also two attics—one used as a boxroom and the other for storing rubbish of every description. Mary opened one of the doors on the second landing, and entered a medium sized room furnished as half bed and half sitting-room. There were basket chairs with soft cushions, an old sofa, a well-stocked book-case, plants on the wide window-ledge and a canary singing his little heart out in a cage above. A small bed in the corner could be hid from view when necessary, a large and very handsome Japanese screen standing at its foot. The floor had no carpet but was polished till it shone like glass and a few rugs were scattered here and there on its surface. The bed was occupied now—a small wasted form, a mass of fair hair, and two bright, very intelligent eyes were all that could be seen from the door. But as Mary came forward there was a quick glad cry of 'Oh! Mary, is that you! How late you are this morning, aren't you!'

Mary went over to the bed and tenderly kissed the wistful little face held up to her. The eldest girl was a true 'mother' to all her brothers and sisters, but this the youngest, the little cripple, was her dearest—her baby.

'Yes, dear, I think I am a little late today. Have you had your breakfast? and did you sleep last night? I hadn't time to come to you sooner, but I know Ursula was with you this morning.'

'Yes, Ursula brought me a cup of tea before she went to Mass—about half-past six—because she knew I had a headache last night, and I have had my breakfast since, so you see I am not neglected. And now, Mary darling! sit down if you can spare a minute at all and tell me all about Clare—a little bird told me she was coming on Thursday,' and the cripple girl's face was all alight with eager sympathy as Mary sat down in a low chair beside her bed and after reading Clare's letter aloud fell to discussing her approaching visit with this the youngest of her flock.

She had been baptised as Angela, but no one ever called her anything but Angel—and if ever the name suited anyone in this poor world, it suited Angela Blake. Seventeen years of age, she had been delicate from her birth and now suffered from a bad spinal curvature and also shortening of one leg. She could get about with a crutch fairly well at times, and had her wheel-chair also, but there were times when she could only manage to get to the sofa in her own room. But a grumble or a complaint was never heard from Angel's lips; she was always bright, always cheerful, and full of interest in the doings of all the others, the comings and goings of these strong healthy ones who were able to go in and out as they pleased and could run and dance and play tennis! Angel often wondered wistfully what it must be like to be strong and straight—but there was no place for envy in her unselfish soul.

She listened now, full of delighted interest, as Mary spoke of their new cousin, wondering what she was like—was she pretty? and would she be good-tempered, or would she be proud and hard to please?

'I like her letter, Angel,' said Mary, 'she has gone through such a hard time lately—first the death of her father and then to lose her fortune, and she was brought up to consider herself so wealthy. We must try to be good to her for she will feel strange amongst us all at first. Angel, you will help me to make her feel at home, I know—won't you dearie? And now I must leave you to dress for I have a lot to do.'

The day passed all too quickly for Mary, and she was fairly tired that night when she found herself at last sitting down for a quiet chat with her father and Tom. They three were alone. Shamus was at a Gaelic meeting. Bride attending one of her numerous committees, and Pat and Nora went off on pleasure bent, while Ursula was upstairs with Angel.

Mr Blake lay back in his armchair, enjoying the luxury of old slippers and an old pipe; Tom was deep in various plans and drawings scattered over the table, and Mary was engaged in what was a very usual task for her—darning the family's socks.

'Father,' she said presently, 'tell me about Clare's mother. She was your younger sister I think? And how did she come to marry a man so different in character and religion to all that she had been used to? It seems so strange in every way!'

Her father was silent for a moment, then he withdrew his pipe slowly from his mouth and sat up in his chair—bracing himself as it seemed to Mary, as if he was going to speak on an unpleasant subject.

'My sister Ursula,' he said at last—'you know Ursula is called after her—went on a visit to some school friends in London, and she met George Castlemaine there. It seems they were mutually attracted almost at once; the man was honest, and good-living, according to his lights, and of course, immensely wealthy. Your aunt wrote and told me all about him.'

He paused for a few minutes and went back to his pipe. His dead sister of long ago had been very dear to James Blake and he seemed to see once more before his eyes the sweet girlish face framed in the soft, dusky hair—sometimes his daughter Ursula reminded him of her, but the living Ursula would never have the beauty and fascination of the other.

Tom had lifted his head from his drawings and was listening quietly.

'I was not surprised when she wrote again,' continued Mr Blake, 'telling me he wanted to marry her, and by the same post came a letter from Castlemaine himself—quite straightforward and honourable, and offering very handsome settlements. There was absolutely nothing against the man except his religion—or, rather, want of religion.'

He paused a moment and smiled as he remarked, 'It's as well Shamus is not here or he would be thinking I should have objected to the man's nationality also. As a matter of fact I did object to it, but still it was a minor consideration in comparison with the religious aspect. Well! I consulted your Uncle Pat, and the upshot of it was that I wrote both to Ursula and George Castlemaine saying that we would agree to the marriage on the condition that any children that might be born to them—either boys or girls—were to be baptised in the Catholic Church and brought up in that faith. We had previously ascertained that the man himself would not entertain for a moment the thought of becoming a Catholic—he was a pronounced Agnostic.'

He paused again and was silent so long that Mary said softly, 'Well! Father?'

'Well, he refused—refused absolutely; said any children of his would not be baptised and would be instructed in no religious dogmas, but that when they were of age they could judge for themselves on religious matters. Of course your Uncle Pat and myself thought that would end the affair once and for all and we wrote to Ursula to come home at once. The next letter told us that she had married George Castlemaine.'

Mary gave a little exclamation, and Tom moved slightly, leaning forward on the table.

'Yes,' went on Mr Blake, 'they were married at the Registry Office and afterwards at a Catholic Church—for which,' he added reverently, 'I thank God. Ursula was just of age, we had no legal control over her and she was evidently completely infatuated with this man. She wrote asking my forgiveness which I could not deny, although I was shocked and hurt beyond words. After her marriage we did not correspond very frequently—she had her own life to live now and it was a different one from ours. I think at first she was happy enough; her husband was quite liberal about her religion and allowed her full freedom in the exercise of her religious duties. It was all right till the child came, but after that I don't think my poor sister knew what happiness was. She wrote to me about that time and her letter was heart-breaking—you can imagine the feelings of a Catholic mother when she looked at her child and knew that it must grow up without the help and comfort of our holy Faith—when she realised that she might never teach her little daughter her first prayers or train the little soul for Heaven. She gave the child private baptism herself—so she told me in one of her letters, and I think she would have managed to have a priest perform the ceremony later, only that she died as you know rather suddenly—within a short time of Clare's birth.'

'Then Clare is baptised, father?'

'Yes; at least as I told you—by private baptism. But she knows absolutely nothing of the Catholic religion—she has received no religious instruction at all.'

'How strange, father! I can hardly imagine such a queer state of things. Oh! I wonder what she will be like?'

'A queer mixture, I should say,' said Tom, speaking for the first time.

'Yes,' agreed Mr Blake, as he knocked the ashes out of his pipe, 'Yes, Tom, a queer mixture as you say. Still I will be glad to see the girl for her mother's sake, and I know I needn't ask you all to be as kind as possible to her—she has gone through her own share of trouble lately! And now I think I'll be off to bed for I am tired and sleepy.'

There was a short silence when he had left the room and then Mary looked across the table at her brother.

'Tom,' she said, 'I feel quite nervous to think of this girl coming amongst us—a sort of pagan evidently in her ideas! And then she is so used to such a different social existence in every way—a large house—perfectly trained servants—an expensive table, and so on. How will we ever get on with her?'

Tom smiled and leaning forward patted the capable hands of the 'housemother'.

'Don't worry, Sis,' he said quietly, 'she knows our circumstances—that we are not overburdened with this world's goods and also that socially we lead a very different life towards that to which she has been accustomed. Surely she will be sensible enough to take us as she finds us.'

Mary sighed, and still looked doubtful.

'There are such a lot of us,' she said with a rueful smile, 'and I only hope we won't frighten her!' Tom laughed cheerfully.

'No fear of that,' he said, 'you may be sure she will be able for the lot of us! I only hope she doesn't prove too much for us to stand!'

Mary rolled up the socks she was darning.

'Well; it's no use worrying or meeting trouble half-way,' she said, 'and I must go and see about a bit of supper for the late ones.'

As she left the room Tom's eyes followed her with a very tender look.

'It would be a queer person that would be afraid of Sis,' he murmured softly, as he gathered his diagrams together, 'God bless her!'

CHAPTER III

'THERE'S A LAND — A DEAR LAND'

Mrs Webb saw Clare Castlemaine off at Euston on the morning she was leaving for Dublin. She was very tearful parting with the girl and Clare also found it hard not to break down. Just a few moments before the train started she noticed on the platform, two young fellows of the usual 'man about town' type; beautifully groomed and wearing the very latest thing in ties and socks, and needless to say looking bored to death. They had been fairly intimate with Clare in that gay social life which she seemed to be leaving behind so quickly now—her partners at many a dance and bridge table; but now she drew back as if to avoid being seen—poor girl she was keenly sensitive at this time, and imagined that everyone was either pitying or sneering at her misfortune.

But Harold Clifford and Jack Grey caught sight of her and came forward at once.

'We heard you were going on a visit to Ireland,' said Harold Clifford, when greetings had been exchanged; 'we came to see a young cousin of mine who was supposed to be leaving by this train, but she has evidently changed her mind and is not going after all. I suppose it is your first visit to the distressful country, Miss Castlemaine? Well, I don't know much about it myself, but Jack here often pays it a visit.'

'Oh! Mr Grey, what is it like? Did you enjoy yourself there?'

Jack Grey laughed.

'I am afraid it would take too long to answer your first question, Miss Castlemaine; but to the other query I can answer with a decided *yes*! But then I have some Irish blood in my veins, I believe, and so I suppose I feel more or less at home there. It may seem a bit strange to you at first.'

'Oh! but my mother was Irish!' cried the girl eagerly.

'Oh! in that case you will be all right! Something in the air will call to the Irish part of you, and before you know where you are you will be "more Irish than the Irish themselves". I have really experienced this myself and so I prophesy that you will enter into your Irish heritage too, and be as happy as the day is long.'

Clare brightened and smiled all over her winsome face.

'Oh! I *hope* so,' she said, 'I have been feeling half afraid you know!'

'Hallo!' said Clifford, 'here are some of your future country folk if I am not greatly mistaken—and as usual at the last minute!'

The train was just on the point of starting when a stout, middle-aged man and woman, gesticulating wildly, were seen racing down the platform, and behind them a young girl, breathless from running, and clasping various rugs and a small portmanteau in her arms.

It was in a corridor carriage and the stout couple were propelled in first with the help of a friendly porter and found seats at a little distance from Clare, but the girl came tumbling in almost on top of her and took the seat opposite, which was the only one vacant. The whistle sounded, there were good wishes from the young men and tearful good-byes from Mrs Webb, and Clare found herself steaming out of Euston.

Her eyes were rather dim as she withdrew them from the window and turned them casually on the girl seated opposite. *Her* eyes bore no traces of tears; they were bright and shining, her whole being radiated happiness, and she seemed too excited to keep still for a moment.

'What a queer girl!' thought Clare, 'I wonder has she suddenly come in for a fortune or something of that sort, that she looks so positively *sparkling* with happiness.' Then she sighed at the thought of the contrast between herself and this girl, and languidly opened one of the numerous magazines with which Mrs Webb had supplied her.

Presently the stout old gentleman came rolling along, and leaning over the seat addressed the girl.

'All right, Mollie?' he asked—and he spoke with the accents of Dublin although Clare did not recognise it as such— 'Faith! that was a near shave! Another minute and we were left behind—and that would have been rather a disappointment to you, eh!'

'*Oh, uncle!* don't *speak* of it!' and the girl's eyes became saucer-like at the bare thought of such a misfortune, 'another day in London I could *not* have endured! Why, I had the very minutes counted!'

The gentleman laughed and went back to his own seat, and Clare found herself looking with renewed interest at Miss Mollie. Why this hurry to leave London? Why had she been counting the very minutes until she escaped from it?

As if in answer to these questioning thoughts the girl caught Clare's eye and smiled suddenly in a most delightful friendly way—she seemed to be bubbling over with good fellowship to all the world.

'Yes, we *had* a narrow squeak, hadn't we?' she remarked, and Clare found herself smiling in sympathy.

'It *would* have been tiresome to have to wait for the night mail,' she agreed.

'Oh! don't mention it!' cried the other in horror, 'when I think of how I have been looking forward to this day, the thought of having to put it off even by a few hours would be too dreadful!'

Clare smiled vaguely; she would have liked to ask the reason for this excitement, but could not bring herself to do so. Her companion, however, did not wait to be asked, but chattered on quite unrestrainedly.

'It is three years since I have been home,' she volunteered, 'I have been in hospital training as a nurse and I always thought it would make me so homesick to go home and then have to come back again, that I never went home for my holidays, just went to some quiet place in England and took a rest. I was so *terribly* homesick when I came to London first—I will never forget it, and I felt I couldn't go through such misery again. And then money was a consideration. I have lived with my uncle and aunt,' giving her head a jerk backwards to indicate the couple behind, 'ever since I was a baby, for I don't remember my own parents, and they—Uncle and Aunt I mean—were quite poor up to lately, but now uncle has come in for an unexpected legacy from America and he will be a fairly rich man now. That is how we are travelling first class,' with a pleased look around—'aren't the carriages lovely and comfortable, and so different from the third!' As Clare had never experienced the latter she only murmured some vague reply, and her fellow traveller went on.

My name is Mollie O'Sullivan, and we live at Rathfarnham—oh! to think that I will really see the dear old spot again in a few hours! I suppose you are going to Dublin, too?'

'Yes,' replied Clare, 'but I am a stranger to Ireland—this is my first visit,' and then to her own surprise she found herself speaking quite freely to this chance acquaintance and telling her all about her impending visit to her Irish relatives and her doubts and fears on the subjects.

Miss O'Sullivan listened with eager sympathy.

'And you have never been in Ireland before!' she exclaimed, and to Clare's amusement her accents expressed boundless pity; 'well, you have a treat in store! Oh! You will like Ireland and the Irish people too—why you are half a Celt yourself, so you are sure to enjoy yourself!'

And Clare remembered that this was the second time that this had been predicted for her.

'I hope so,' she said, but her voice was still doubtful.

The journey to Holyhead passed pleasantly and agreeably—thanks to her little Irish friend. 'Uncle Tim' and 'Aunt Mary' were brought forward and introduced; they proved to be as chatty and gay as their niece and Clare found herself coming out of her shell and talking to these people without a vestige of that impenetrable English reserve with which she had always encased herself on other railway journeys.

She mentioned something of this to Miss O'Sullivan in a half laughing manner.

'Oh, yes, I know what you mean,' was the reply, 'the better classes in England are all like that; it must be amusing to watch them on a journey—so stiff and prim especially of course the women—suspicious of everyone. And then the lower classes—why they go to the other extreme! Really the contemplation of "'Arry and 'Arriet," travelling—say on a bank holiday—must make the angels weep! Heaven be praised, that we have no prototype of them in Ireland.'

Clare laughed a little.

'You have a poor opinion of the English people, I am afraid,' she said.

'I have been three years amongst them,' replied the other speaking in a more serious tone than usual. 'And I have seen the best and the worst side of their character, as we nurses always do. As a whole I do not like them—I don't mind saying this to you now that I know you are half Irish yourself—but I *did* meet a few I sincerely liked. But they were all amongst the nurses themselves. I have never yet seen the English *man* I could admire—I found it hard enough to even tolerate the average English male!' Then Mollie laughed merrily.

'No matter!' she cried gaily, 'I have left them and their gloomy country behind—for ever, I hope! Oh! the joy to be really going *home*! I simply can't realise it!'

Clare was amused and also surprised at her companion's talk. She had been brought up to regard England and the English as *the* nation par excellence—the very salt of the earth—and to consider her mixture of Irish blood as something that was at least to be regretted—something best not spoken about. And now here was the Irish aspect presented to her—the Celtic contempt for poor John Bull shown to her by the frank criticism of this Irish girl with the clever face and clear grey eyes.

On the mail boat she noticed the various soft brogues around her and to her own ears her voice when she spoke seemed to suddenly sound several notes too high and shrill. She felt annoyed, but the fact remained.

It was a glorious September evening as they steamed into Kingstown Harbour, and Clare was astonished at the beauty of Dublin Bay and at Kingstown itself, which with its pavilion and gardens, terraces and fine houses and pretty villas, its numerous church spires—all glorified in the light of the setting sun—made up a picture not easily forgotten. She gazed with delight at the scenery of the harbour and noticed all the different vessels from the large steamers and mail boats to the smaller pleasure craft and dainty yachts, resting like large white birds on the surface of the calm water. In the near distance could be seen Dalkey and Killiney with all their picturesque environment.

Clare had often heard the words of Lady Dufferin's well-known song:

> 'Oh! Bay of Dublin, my mind you are troublin'
> Your beauty haunts me like a fevered dream.'

But never till now had she realised their true meaning. She was so engrossed in her thoughts that they were quite close to the landing stage before she knew it. Turning round she noticed Mollie O'Sullivan. The girl was standing behind her, but she seemed quite unconscious of Clare's presence, her eyes were fixed on the nearing shore, and the tears were falling on her clasped hands. Clare turned aside quickly, feeling that she had no right to look upon a soul so moved, and a thought came quickly into her mind—almost against her wish—'Why! if I was thirty years away from England, instead of only three, I could never feel like that! What love after all the Irish must have for their country!'

They were alongside in another moment, and Clare stood waiting her turn to go down the gangway having given her luggage in charge of one of the sailors. She gazed eagerly down at the small crowd waiting to greet the passengers, wondering which of her relatives would come to meet her. Then her turn came; 'Mind yourself, Miss! Hold my hand—that's it now!' and she was safely down the gangway. The next minute she was accosted by a tall, thin gentleman of middle age, who lifting his hat, said interrogatively:

'Is it Miss Castlemaine?'

'Yes, I am Clare Castlemaine,' replied Clare, looking up eagerly to meet the gaze of a pair of kind eyes, 'and you are Uncle James I am sure!' and she found her hands held in a warm grasp.

'You are welcome, my dear—very welcome, both for your dear mother's sake and for your own,' said Mr Blake with deep feeling in his tones, and then he added in a lighter strain; 'We were not quite sure of you—there was another tall girl in black and Tom and I were nearly making a bet on it! I thought *you were you*, and he thought *you were she!*' and Mr Blake laughed at his own joke.

Then glancing round at his son he went on:

'And this is Tom, my dear—your cousin Clare, my boy. I hope you two will be good friends, but indeed you must be good friends with us all. And now is this the man with your handwraps?—That's right. We may as well take our seats, but there is always a little wait for the mails you know—your other luggage will be in the van all right.'

So talking he piloted her to the train, drawn up alongside the pier, and Clare feeling already that she would like this new uncle, found herself presently sitting beside him and opposite Tom. She took a good look at her cousin now, and was surprised to find him very intelligent looking, quietly dressed, and—as she afterwards discovered—possessed of a perfect manner. She had an idea at the back of her head that all Irishmen—young ones anyway—must of necessity be a bit rakish and wild and always making jokes. Tom turned from the window and met her inquiring gaze. He leant forward with a slight smile—'Well! I hope your scrutiny will end in a favourable verdict?' he said, with a twinkle of the eye. Clare coloured and laughed, and the ice was broken. By the time Westland Row was reached the trio were like old friends.

She saw little of the city during the drive to Rathmines—she was too excited to take much notice of her surroundings. Was not every moment bringing her nearer to all these unknown cousins? Her uncle and Tom were all right certainly, but perhaps they were exceptions? What about the girls of the family?—the eldest Miss Blake must be years older than herself—she might be cold and reserved, might not want the visit of an unknown English cousin, at all! How Tom Blake would have smiled to himself if he could have read his cousin's thoughts. Here they were at last! What a tall old house, and a lot of steps up to it! Her legs are trembling a little as she mounts these same steps but before she can reach the topmost, the hall door is flung open. Clare sees a vista of a large dark hall that seems to her excited fancy to be full of people—and right enough the whole Blake family had managed to be at home on this evening to welcome the new cousin—then the next moment someone comes forward from all the rest and Clare sees a sweet Madonna-like face, and hears one of the sweetest voices she has ever heard, saying:

'Welcome a hundred times, dear Clare! We are all *so* glad to see you!' and soft lips touched her cheek.

The next moment she is surrounded, and kissed and hugged by the girls, and has her hand nearly shaken off by the boys. The Blakes never did things by halves, and they had taken to Clare at once. Instead of a cold and haughty young English girl with a supercilious stare—the kind of vision they had been rather dreading—they beheld a pretty slight girl with fluffy, fair hair, and a very wistful look in her blue eyes—'Something like a lost dog, you know!'—Pat remarked later, to the disgust of his romantic brother Shamus.

Mary rescued Clare at last and took her upstairs to the room prepared for her. Very sweet and dainty the spare-room looked—and well it might—after all the various 'finishing touches' and general brightening up to which it had been subjected by Mary's deft hands.

Nevertheless, she looked round it now a little doubtfully, all fresh and clean no doubt, but how different it must be to the luxurious bedroom—with probably a dressing-room and boudoir also—to which doubtless her cousin had been accustomed.

'I hope you will be comfortable here,' she said, rather wistfully; 'it is the best I could manage for you Clare, but I know that you were used to——'

But Clare interrupted her swiftly.

'Oh! Mary! *please!* Don't. If you only knew how glad in many ways I was to leave London and how delighted I am to be with you! And you are all so kind to me—I feel almost at home already! And do you know I felt quite nervous coming amongst you all—if only I had known how kind you all were!'

Mary put her arms round her and kissed her with real affection.

'Oh! what a relief it is to hear you speak like that!' she said, and then she laughed her rather rare but hearty laugh. 'If you knew how I have been dreading *you*! We were all a bit afraid at the thought of you, but I think I was the worst! But see how mistaken we all were. And now I will leave you for a while—there is hot water and all you want here—and I'll come back and bring you down to tea then,' and she was gone, leaving Clare to her own reflections.

They were fairly pleasant ones too, as she washed her face and hands and smoothed her hair. Her new relations seemed really glad to see her, her welcome had been a sincere one, and it had reached the very heart of the girl, for lately she had been inclined to retreat into her shell and to turn a hard face to the world which had treated her so coldly.

But here amongst her mother's people all seemed different and Clare began to feel that she had really come to *a home*.

'I wonder what I should wear?' she debated in some perplexity—'*tea*—Mary said, but it is just seven o'clock! Well, I suppose a tea-gown will do,' and she slipped into what she considered a very simple affair of black lace.

Soon afterwards, Mary's knock sounded at the door, and when Clare opened it she noticed that her cousin glanced at her dress in some surprise.

Clare went to the point at once with her usual directness.

'Mary,' she said—'I didn't know exactly what to do in the way of dress. Is this all right—or should I have dressed for dinner?'

Mary laughed, and slipped her arm through Clare's as she answered gaily.

'Dressed for dinner! No, indeed! We don't dine late. You see, except for myself, they are all out through the day and they get a light lunch in town—then we have a sort of high tea about seven o'clock. Your dress is lovely, but everyone will be afraid to talk to you—you are so grand!'

They had reached the dining-room now where tea—a substantial meal with several additional items in honour of the guest—was ready.

Mr Blake came forward and drew Clare to the table. Placing her beside himself, the others took their seats and the meal began, but not before there had been a moment's silence, and Clare in astonishment saw the sign of the cross made reverently by all at the table. Then came the cheerful rattle of tea cups, the sound of knives and forks and gay chatter and laughter.

Clare had never experienced anything quite like it before—the gay nonsensical talk, the happy joking, and above all the swift repartee that went on with such real good nature.

'I am afraid you will think I have a very unruly family, Clare,' said her uncle, smiling at her over his glasses as he carved the ham, 'but they are not as bad as they seem!'

'Now, Dad!' interposed Pat, 'don't be putting Clare against us—and she doesn't even know us yet! I don't believe she knows one of us from the other! Now do you, Clare?'

Clare shook her head, and smilingly had to admit that she was a bit puzzled as to the identity of most of her new cousins.

'Allow me then to give you a short—a very short category of the esteemed members of your family, now assembled around this sumptuous board.'

'Ah! Pat, be quiet, and let Clare take her tea in peace!'

'Mary, I must really beg that you will not interrupt in this rude manner! Now Clare, you have met Tom—all I need say about him is, don't let him bully you or give you good advice—you needn't try to look important, old man—we all know you! Then there is your cousin Ursula in the next seat—I am taking them as they are placed at table as you will observe, it will save any amount of jealousy as to who should be mentioned first and so on! Now she looks very sedate and quiet, doesn't she? You think so?—yes. Oh! Well, I will only answer with the well-known phrase of "wait and see!" And now let me introduce your cousin Bride, merely adding that should you desire any information as to the social conditions of the Irish poor—and you might like to contribute articles on these subjects to the English press, its quite the fashion now-a-days—as to how many herrings they eat at dinner—or what day of the week can they afford the luxury of pig's cheek, also any details you want in regard to our schools, social clubs, free breakfasts, homes for aged females, for inebriated males, for——'

'Imbecile youths,' interposed Bride, 'and I must see if I can find a vacancy there for a near relative of my own.'

'Or any other social problem,' went on Pat, as if no interruption had occurred, 'you can safely refer in all these matter to my sister Bride.' He cleared his throat and glanced down the table. 'And now behold!' with a wave of the hand towards Nora, 'see our Society beauty—our lovely gad-a-bout! One of the noted belles of Rathmines! The'—but here his speech was momentarily checked by a hard crust dexterously aimed by Nora and landing on his nose.

'Shut up for goodness' sake!' said that young lady. 'Dad! Can't you tell him to hold his tongue for once?'

'Oh! Listen! listen! to her dulcet tones!' said Pat, gazing with simulated admiration at her flushed countenance, 'behold, the soft blush mount to her girlish brow. Oh! that Gerald Hammond was but here to see it! Or Ronnie Black, or Charlie Daly, or——'

'There, that will do, Pat; leave your sister in peace—don't tease her any more,' interposed Mr Blake, taking pity on Nora's speechless indignation.

'Very well, sir! Let us pass on and leave this blushing subject for a while. Now Clare, take a good look at your cousin Shamus, for in him you see the new spirit of the age—the reincarnation of the Celt—the great revival of the Gael! Has he spoken to you yet? No? I thought not. He would not condescend to speak your Saxon tongue—the very accents would choke him!'

Clare looked half fearfully at Shamus—how much of Pat's talk was serious she did not know.

To her relief Shamus smiled back and answered in remarkably good English—the soft modulated English to which she was already becoming accustomed—

'Don't mind that mad fellow, Clare—when he's done his nonsense *we* will give *you his* character.'

'*My* character is it? Well you know that it is pure as the undriven snow, as high as Mont Pelier, as untarnished as gold, as good as—as——'

'Oh! stop, for for pity's sake!' interposed Bride, 'do you want Clare to think us *all* mad?'

'Not *all*—not all, my dear sister—only a certain portion of us!'

'I think I know you all now,' said Clare smiling, 'but'—with a sudden recollection of a loving little scrawl at the foot of her uncle's letter, 'which of you is Angel?'

'Angel!' repeated Tom, and 'Angel!' cried some of the others.

Then Mary spoke.

'I will bring you to see Angel after tea,' she said, 'she thought you would be tired or I would have brought you to her sooner. She was not feeling very well and did not come downstairs this evening.'

Clare, who of course, knew nothing about Angel, and thought it was perhaps a headache from which she was suffering, now asked gaily of Pat to give her Angel's character also. To her surprise Pat only smiled and his blue eyes had a strangely tender look as he replied—

'Angel's character? Well, Angel is just our little bit of Heaven!—but you will see for yourself!'

And in a short while Clare found herself with Mary going towards Angel's room. As they went Mary told Clare in a few short but tender words about Angel's health, and when they entered the room and Clare saw the eager little form on the sofa, with the wistful eyes but bright smile, her heart went out to this little crippled cousin, and she went forward swiftly and put her arms tenderly round the poor shrunken body.

'And so you are Angel,' she said, 'and it was you that added the little line of invitation to Uncle's letter? Do you know, I think it was that dear little scribble at the end that really made me decide to come over to Ireland!'

'Oh, *was* it? I *am* glad!' and Angel's eyes were shining, 'do sit down—take that armchair and we will have a chat. I've been dying to see you, but I wanted you to have your tea first.'

Mary had slipped away and Clare drawing up her chair close to Angel's couch listened to the innocent chatter and gladly answered her eager questions.

Two or three of the others strolled in after a while, and then came Mr Blake, and it was delightful to see the love that existed between Angel and her father. It brought the sudden tears to Clare's eyes, and she had to bite her lips hard to keep from breaking down. But Mary noticed her and tactfully drew her attention away, talking of other things with such delicate kindness and consideration that Clare soon found herself chatting away at her ease once more.

But she was really tired, more from the mental than the physical strain of the day, and she was glad to accept Mary's suggestion and retire early to bed. Her cousin accompanied her to her room to see that she had everything she wanted and to wish her a real good-night.

Left alone, Clare glanced casually round the room—which she had not noticed in detail earlier in the evening—and her gaze was arrested by a picture of Our Lady under her title of 'Mother of Perpetual Succour.' The strange old-world look of the picture aroused her interest and she examined it more closely.

'What a queer picture!' she murmured. 'It seems very old—a relic of mediæval times I suppose. "Mother of Perpetual Succour,"' she repeated slowly. 'What a strange title. But how comforting to those who can believe in such things,—fancy a Mother of Perpetual Succour! Oh, what peace and joy the very thought of such a thing would bring to one's heart, but not for me—not for me. And yet my own mother believed in all these old superstitions—and I suppose my cousins do also. How strange it is to see how these old beliefs still survive,' and with a half smile, half sigh, she began to prepare for rest.

CHAPTER IV

ST COLUMBA'S HOME

Should old acquaintance be forgot.

In the dining-room of St Columba's Home for district nurses, the staff were assembled round the breakfast table, awaiting the entrance of the Matron for that meal to commence. It was a large bare room, containing little furniture besides the long dining table with the chairs placed primly around; there were a few old paintings on the wall—the gift of the women of title whose town house this once had been—and at a small side table stood two of the junior nurses ready to serve the bacon. Two large loaves are on the table, and two equal quantities of butter—one at each end of the board. At the Matron's end is the tea-tray, and two brown teapots, and on the lid of one of those sits a small and exceedingly antiquated cosy, which never by any amount of stretching or of squeezing could be made to go over the tea-pot.

At the opposite end of the table are the two staff nurses, and on each side stand the probationers—trained nurses all, but doing their probationary period in district work. They have, most of them, been to seven-thirty Mass at a city church near the Home, but a few lazy ones amongst them have not been out. The Matron has not returned from the church yet.

'Stir the tea quickly—someone!' exclaimed Nurse Dunbar.

The nurse nearest to the tea-tray whips away the useless cosy, and lifting the lid of the teapot commences to stir the contents vigorously, until one of the others exclaims—'Here's Matron!' whereupon she bangs back the lid and almost drops the spoon as she scurries back to her seat.

Miss McFarland enters almost immediately, grace is said, the nurses drop into their places and the meal commences.

Two of the nurses cut the bread and hand it round, the two at the side table dispense a minute rasher of bacon to each nurse, and the Matron pours out the tea. Two or three of the nurses who happen to be especially fond of their morning cup, watch her anxiously, for Miss McFarland has a most extraordinary way of dealing with the teapot—if tea can be spoiled in the pouring out, she will certainly manage to spoil it. She splashes it into the cups, holding the teapot aloft until the fluid poured out more nearly resembles a glass of 'Guinness' than the 'cup that cheers'; when the pot is half empty she deluges it with water, and then pours the contents of the two teapots backwards and forwards in some unique manner, so that in the end each nurse received a cup of the queerest concoction that was ever dispensed under the name of tea.

To crown all, one of the staff had overslept herself, and her tea had been poured out by mistake.

'Oh, is Nurse Johnson not down yet? Well! just pass me back her cup please!' and the contents of the cup, milk and all, is flung into the teapot as a finishing touch to the beverage.

The meal is over in about twenty minutes, and the nurses troop away to get ready for the day's work.

'Matron is making the lotion worse than ever,' one of them remarks to her companion as they mount the long flight of stairs to the bedroom. By this name is the morning tea known amongst themselves.

'Oh! awful!' replied the other, 'we used to say that it was tea one in a hundred, but indeed it is getting more like one in a thousand now!'

They leave the house in twos and threes, going to their various districts. Of the two staff nurses, the senior takes the most recent probationer to initiate her into the ways of 'slumming,' and the other staff nurse—Mary Carmichael—sets off alone for her morning's work. She has a large district in the Coombe vicinity—a good distance from St Columba's, for the Home is situated in one of the old squares on the north side of the city.

Mary Carmichael was about thirty years of age, of medium height, and with a rather slight figure, good eyes and hair and a clear complexion. She was not particularly good-looking, and neither was she plain, but she varied greatly in her appearance; at times she looked almost pretty, and again there were occasions on which she seemed really plain. Her looks depended to a great extent on her feelings—happiness could nearly make a beauty of her, but sorrow ravaged her good looks with a sweeping hand.

And Mary had seen much trouble during her life. The meaning of the word home was almost unknown to her, for being left an orphan very young she had been bandied about by various relatives until she had been able to earn her own living. At the earliest age allowable she entered one of the large hospitals in London, where she stayed for four years; then she did private nursing for some time in a surgical home in the West End, and after that she took up District work, and for the last two years had been one of the staff nurses at St Columba's.

Here she was completely happy, for she loved her work, and had found her true vocation in the slums. To Mary it was sheer delight to go in and out of the alleys and lanes grouped round St Patrick's, and her whole heart was given to her daily toil amongst the poor of her native city.

She was a strange mixture, and yet few guessed the various elements that were sometimes at war within her. Most of her ordinary friends and fellow nurses would have been amazed if they could have known that there were times when Mary Carmichael felt inclined to fling her district bag away to the far ends of the earth, and leave the stern path of duty to lead a life of frivolity and pleasure, to wear beautiful clothes and to eat and drink of the best, to travel where she wished on this fair earth of ours—and to flirt and sing and dance her way through life. When these temptations—as she regarded them—came to her, she would pray harder, work harder, and impose upon herself something in the way of penance, until she 'came back to her senses'—as she expressed it. But in the past it was not so. Mary had been a convert to the Church for the last five years, but before that time, religion of any kind had been a dead letter to her, and she had lived her life her own way, only trying to get the best she could out of it—not that she had ever done anything seriously wrong, but looking back now with clearer eyes, she often wondered how it was that she had managed to keep on the straight path. The young Irish girl in London, full of life and gaiety, and knowing little of the real evils of that modern Babylon, had several times been very nearly swept away in the currents of the fast life all around her. She saw other nurses going that way—especially in the West End Home where she worked for some time—teas, theatres, supper parties, trips up the river, dinners at Richmond—all these first. Then came week-end trips and soon good-bye to the drudgery of the nursing profession, and heigh-ho for a life of pleasure, for a few years of luxury—for a draught from that cup which is so intoxicating, until—the dregs are reached—and then for the bitterness which is worse than death, for remorse unspeakable and for the worm which dieth not. Yet somehow, Mary had kept straight, and still managed to enjoy herself fully. No one flung herself with more zest into the enjoyment of a Bohemian supper, or the abandon of a masked ball, or a 'joy ride' to Richmond, than Mary Carmichael, and yet she never allowed the men of the party to take the slightest liberty with her—she was one of those women who always wield a certain fascination for the other sex, but who always manage to command their respect also.

And then suddenly had come the awakening. A casual visit to a little Catholic Church down Soho way while a 'Mission' was in progress, a certain sermon which kept her awake all that night and many succeeding ones—further attendance at the Mission, followed by more wakeful nights, and general misery, and finally an interview with one of the missioners, a course of religious instruction—and her reception into the Church. A new world dawned for Mary Carmichael then. With the zeal of the convert, she flung herself heart and soul, into the arena of the Church militant—she worked and fasted, and prayed—her old haunts knew her no more. With her adherence to the old Faith, came also the wish to return to her native city again, so she entered St Columba's Home, and after her probationary period was passed, she still remained there as Staff nurse. A daily communicant, a Child of Mary, a temperance pioneer, a worker in every social scheme for uplifting and helping the poor and the sinning, such was Mary Carmichael now. And to all outward seeming her religion and her work filled her life.

But Mary herself knew better, she knew that her 'other self' was yet strong within her. She was an ardent theatregoer still, a great lover of the picture houses, and all kinds of amusements, and never missed a dance, if she could manage it at all. Sometimes her conscience pricked her about these things, but she would persuade herself that they were all innocent pleasures, and that she surely needed some relaxation, some little contrast to the strenuous work, some relief from the scenes of sordid poverty, amidst which her days were spent. All of which was true, but she could never quite harden her heart to 'the still small voice' which reminded her now and then of that other self which she knew she possessed—that self which loved the world, and the flesh, and had to be kept under with those powerful weapons which are found in their real strength only within the fold of the Catholic Church—'for these kind goeth not forth but by prayer and fasting.'

But lately Mary had not been troubled by her spiritual condition, and neither had she been as keen as usual in the pursuit of amusement. A great happiness was dawning for her, a something that seemed too good to be true, was drawing near to her. She who had seen men at their worst, and who had so often seen the beast that is in every man, rise to the surface and confront her in all its hideous nakedness, so that she had almost despaired of every meeting one who was clean-souled and pure hearted—was at last compelled to admit that her ideal man had entered her life. For years she had mistrusted nearly every man she met—at most she held them in contempt. This by the way did not prevent her flirting with them—flirtation came naturally to Mary, and even now in her regenerate days she could seldom resist an innocent flirtation when a favourable occasion occurred, but she looked upon it as a game of give and take, and she was well able to look after herself at the same game. But so far, she had never regarded her dealings with men in a serious light; the years in London had taught her to take care of herself, to enjoy herself, and to get all the amusement she could while with the opposite sex, but they had also taught her to regard them as woman's natural enemy—ready at any moment to take an advantage if it came within their power. She had gone to London very young and innocent—a mere child in the knowledge of good and evil—and disillusionment had come so quickly and so thoroughly that although the Catholic religion now taught her that men can be good and pure and clean—still the old memories of what she had seen and heard and learned while working in London remained with her and more or less coloured her views of men for all time.

But at last she had met a man who could command all her respect and whom she could honour and look up to with reverence. For two years she had known Dr Delaney and the more she knew of him, the more she honoured him. That their friendship was quickly merging into something nearer and dearer she knew too—and there were times when Mary almost refused to believe that he could care for her; her woman's instinct told her the truth, but her great love made her humble and in her own eyes she appeared unworthy of him. At such times she could have gone down on her knees and 'thanked God fasting for a good man's love.'

From house to house she went swiftly, for she had a heavy morning's work before her, and that each nurse should be in time for the two o'clock dinner was as a law of the Medes and Persians in St Columba's Home. Hurrying down Francis Street she almost collided with a tall girl in a neat tailor-made costume who was emerging from one of the side alleys.

'What, Bride!' she exclaimed gladly, 'how are you? You and I should meet in heaven—we meet so often in this part of the world.'

Bride Blake laughed. 'I was just thinking of you, Mary!' she cried, 'I want to give you a case—listen till I tell you'—and she went into rapid details for Mary's benefit, and the latter listened and made a note of the name and address as she said gaily, 'I will never want for cases, Bride, while you are slumming—you give me enough of them.'

Bride smiled ruefully. 'Yes, I know dear,' she said, 'but I really can't help it. Somehow you can do such a lot more than I can for the poor souls, and then I don't know whether it is some magic that the uniform possesses or what, but I do know that you are always welcome, and I—well my welcome is sometimes a bit uncertain.'

'It's the uniform of course,' said Mary, laughing. 'Who could resist it? Well! I must be off—I haven't any spare time this morning.'

'Oh, wait a minute,' cried Bride, 'our English cousin, Clare Castlemaine—you remember me telling you that we expected her?—arrived last Thursday.'

'Oh! did she really! Well, and what is the verdict?'

'Far better than we anticipated—quite a nice girl, and not a bit of a swank, as the boys express it. Come out tonight and be introduced—will you?'

'I'm sorry Bride, but I can't tonight—I'm going to the opera.'

'Oh! with Dr Delaney, I suppose? Lucky girl, and its *Faust* too! Well, I won't keep you; come any evening you can—you know how welcome you always are.' And with a smile and a nod Bride was off to look up a defaulting 'mother' who had been absent from her baby club for the last few weeks, and needed to be brought back to a realisation of her duty.

Mary Carmichael got through her morning's work and reached St Columba's with just five minutes in which to change from bonnet and cloak to cap and apron and to generally tidy herself for dinner. Her room was at the top of the house and the stairs from the hall upwards counted a hundred. But she sped up them two at a time, breathless, but radiant.

She shared her bedroom with Nurse Johnson, who was engaged in an anxious survey of herself in front of the glass as Mary entered.

'Hallo, Carmichael!' she said, without turning round, 'that you? Do you know I've discovered two more freckles on my nose!'

'Really,' said Mary, busily pulling out drawers and searching for a missing stud. 'I'm sure it's all those face creams and things—Oh! here it is, thank goodness!—that you are always rubbing on that develop those blemishes to your beauty!'

'Don't be a sarcastic idiot, Carmichael,' was the polite retort, 'and don't get flustered, we've plenty of time, there's three minutes yet.'

But as if to prove her a prevaricator of the truth, the dinner bell sounded at that moment—it had been cracked for some time now, and the reverberations it gave out were exasperating and discordant.

'There now!' exclaimed Mary, as she stuck a cap-pin in anyhow; 'I must fly! It's all very well for you, but I'm supposed to set an example,' and she left the room hastily, the click of her little heels down the stone stairs coming back to Nurse Johnson as she remained placidly arranging her hair and fixing on her cap. Not till the last hair was in place, and the cap at just the correct angle that suited her best, did she leave the room and leisurely descend the stair, to enter the dining-room just as the soup was being removed.

'Late again, Miss Johnson!' said Miss McFarland; but she spoke as one resigned to the inevitable, for Nurse Johnson's term of probation was nearly over, and she was hardly ever known to be punctual in her comings or goings or for her meals or lectures. The other nurses often wondered how on earth she had managed to get through her hospital training.

The meals at St Columba's had not much variety about them; four days out of the seven the dinner consisted of roast mutton brought to table ready cut into slices and floating in tepid watery gravy—and always seeming to taste quite different from meat cut straight from the joint. There was a meat pie on one day of the week—to use up the scraps of other days—corned beef on Sundays, and fish, of course, on Fridays. They got fairly good soup and generally a pudding of some kind—not always—a day would come now and then when the cook would be 'put out' over something, and on these occasions, after the removal of the meat, Anne, the elderly housemaid—who was a regular character in herself, having acted as ward-maid in most of the Dublin Hospitals, and thereby 'knowing a thing or two,' as she expressed it—would stoop down and whisper mysteriously into the matron's ear, whereupon that lady would proclaim as though in pained surprise.

'Oh, really! no pudding today! Dear me! Well you nurses will have to get your tea earlier, that's all.'

As the tea was brought up every day at half-past three the nurses being due on their districts again at half-past four, it was generally understood amongst them that Miss McFarland said this simply for the sake of saying something.

After dinner they were free until they left the house for their evening round. Supper was at eight o'clock, and any nurse who wanted to go out after that meal, had to ask permission, except it was her evening off duty.

They generally gathered together in the large room at the back of the house used as a recreation room, during the short time of leisure between dinner and going on duty again, and free from the restraint of the matron's presence, they could talk and laugh and 'talk shop' to their hearts' content.

Nurse Johnson usually reclined gracefully on the sofa and Nurse Seely, her greatest chum, would sit beside her, and they would talk confidentially on the subjects dearest to them both. Nurse Ferguson, a typical hard-featured and harsh-tongued Northern, who always look well after No. 1, generally managed to appropriate the corner seat on the fireside couch for herself, the two staff nurses had the arm-chairs delegated to them, and the juniors found seats for themselves as best they could, the two most junior—in other words the two who had been the shortest time at the Home—had to cut the bread and butter and hand round the tea to the others.

Daisy Ray was the other staff nurse, and she and Mary Carmichael sat together chatting, for they had many interests in common, although they were not at all alike in character. Daisy

Ray was a small doll-like little person very good-tempered and talkative, but with a fund of sound common-sense. She was engaged to be married to Brendan Kelly, a very decent young fellow in a government appointment, and they were only waiting for the promised 'rise' in his salary to set up house together.

The telephone rang in the corridor outside—its sharp ting just making itself heard above the nurses' chatter, and one of the juniors answering it, came back to say that Nurse Carmichael was wanted.

Nurse Carmichael, her colour rising a little, left the room. Before she took up the receiver she guessed who was ringing her up.

'Hallo?'

'Hallo! Oh, is that you? How are you?'

'Very fit, thanks. All right yourself? Good! What about tonight, will it be alright?'

'Yes, of course, it is my evening off. Where will we meet—same place as usual?'

'Yes, top of Grafton Street; quarter to eight. I think I've got fairly decent seats.'

'All right, I'll be there.'

'And—are you there?—don't forget your latch-key—and be in time!'

'As if I was ever late! Don't *you* keep *me* waiting, that's more likely!'

'Well, goodbye till then. I have a crowd of patients to see yet.'

'Well, get them through before tonight. Goodbye, till we meet!'

Mary hung up the receiver and smiled to herself happily. Even the sound of his voice over the telephone stirred all her being with joy unspeakable. Oh! but this man was very dear to her!

She came back slowly and sat down beside Daisy Ray, who glanced up at her with a quiet smile.

'That was Dr Delaney, I suppose,' she said, 'and, of course, I remember now this is your evening off. Are you going out, Mac?' for by this abbreviation was Mary known to her chosen friends amongst the nurses.

She smiled back at Daisy. 'Yes,' she said, 'we are going to see *Faust* and oh, Ray dear, I feel I am going to have a simply scrumptious time!'

On her evening 'off' Mary had no visits to pay, so she sat down and wrote letters when the other nurses had dispersed, and that duty accomplished, she settled herself comfortably with a book till after six o'clock, when she descended carefully and quietly to the kitchen premises. Only the two staff nurses were allowed into the kitchen at St Columba's and they were only supposed to go down with messages from the matron or on some business of that sort. Tea in the kitchen was strictly prohibited, but, needless to say, for that very reason it was indulged in as often as could be managed. This depended greatly upon what state of mind the cook would happen to be in, and also on what nurse asked for the privilege, for cook had her favourites, like others, but among them Mary Carmichael might be safely reckoned, so once safely in the kitchen without encountering the matron on her perilous way thither, she knew that she would get her tea all right.

Martha, the cook, was a stout woman with small suspicious eyes, and a suspicious mind also. She had an uncertain temper, and was held in awe by most of the staff at St Columba's, with the exception of Anne, the housemaid, who, according to her own words, could 'hould her own with the ould boy himself.'

Martha was in the best of humour this evening, Anne was not present, and peace reigned.

Mary was soon pouring out tea 'that would stand of itself' and enjoying hot buttered toast.

'Cook, you are a dear,' she said, 'this is the only decent cup of tea I ever get in St Columba's, and only for you this evening I would have had to go down to the D.B.C. It's such a nuisance supper not being till eight o'clock, and nothing allowed between!'

'Well! that's true, God knows! It's often I pity ye all, with such long fasts between meals. Drink up that tea now, its fine and strong and will stand to ye. I suppose 'tis to the theatre that ye'ill be going to?'

'Yes, cook. The opera is on you know— *Faust*. Well, thanks ever so much—you're a jewel; but I must go and dress now.' And, mounting the long flights of stairs once again she entered her bedroom, and was speedily discarding her uniform and dressing for the evening. She brushed out the soft masses of hair, and arranged it again in a more elaborate style than was allowed in uniform, sponged her face and hands, and slipped on a dainty underskirt and camisole. She changed her stockings too, and put on pretty shoes, for Mary was particular over the small details of her toilet, which was one reason why she always gave one the impression of a well-dressed woman. Then came the black evening skirt, the dressy blouse, with the little finishing touches to her hair—the little dash of powder on her face, the cobweb of a handkerchief breathing violets which shared her theatre bag with her purse and—the latch-key!

As she flung the latter in and shut the bag with a hurried little snap, she said, half aloud, 'I didn't forget you this time, anyway!'

Then she got into her long coat, drew a motor veil over her head, and taking up a pair of long gloves in her hand, went downstairs.

Daisy Ray had come in from the district and was in the sitting-room when Mary looked in for a moment on her way out, and she greeted the latter with a smile. Mary stood in the doorway fastening her gloves and Nurse Ray exclaimed, 'You do look nice, Mac! Are you off now? Well! have a good time! and give my love to Theodore,' she called after her friend's retreating figure.

Dr Delaney was waiting at the top of Grafton Street when Mary got there. She recognised him while she was still some distance away. He was very tall and slight, and looked very well in his light overcoat and silk muffler. He had brown eyes with a very slight cast in them—only noticeable at times, and especially when he was at all excited or annoyed—his hair, although he was still under forty, was thickly sprinkled with grey, and a slight moustache hid a rather weak mouth.

He came forward now, lifting his hat, as Mary approached, and smiling down on her with the half whimsical half affectionate look which always made her heart beat a little faster.

'I'm not late, am I?' she asked as they shook hands.

'No. Indeed for a wonder I think you are fairly well up to time! I was just wondering whether I would have time to finish this cigarette?'

Mary laughed. 'Smoke it as we go along,' she said, 'I don't want to miss the overture.'

They sauntered towards the theatre in the midst of a crowd of others going the same way; couples walking like themselves, the ladies in theatre wraps and with motor veils or scarves thrown round their hair—others driving up in carriages or motors.

'Have you got your latch-key?' asked Dr Delaney. This was a standing joke with them, for several times Mary had been late at an appointment through leaving her key at the Home, and having to race back for it when she was perhaps half-way to the meeting place. The idea of daring to *ring* at the sacred portal at such a late hour as her return would be never entered her head. Miss McFarland was a light sleeper and anyone who made the slightest noise when coming in late would be sure to hear of it next morning. Some sarcastic allusions would be made to 'fairy footsteps,' and so on, and the unfortunate culprit would writhe in silence at the breakfast table.

Mary laughed now as she answered, 'Yes, I have it safe this time.'

'Do you know that I knew you were coming before I saw you,' he said suddenly.

'What do you mean?' said Mary, 'How could you know that?'

'I don't know—but I was standing just there at the bicycle shop and I *felt*—there is no other way to describe it—that you were coming round the corner just as you appeared.'

Mary laughed rather unsteadily. 'Telepathy, I suppose,' she said, and just then they reached the theatre.

It was filling rapidly, but they had good seats in the parterre. The overture was just beginning and as Mary divested herself of her coat and leant back in her seat she felt that she was going to have a good time.

Such hours come to us now and then in a lifetime, when we seem to be completely happy—hours that will come like an oasis in the desert, times when we are able to put black care behind us, to forget the worry of the days gone by, and when we remember not the burden of tomorrow awaiting for us. Such an hour was Mary's this night and she enjoyed every minute of the time. The opera was one of her favourites, both she and Dr Delaney knew it well and listened with keen appreciation to every note of Gounod's masterpiece. They exchanged confidences and criticisms and incidentally ate chocolate during the intervals, and when at last it was over, Mary fetched a little sigh of regret.

'Well, did you enjoy it?' asked her companion as they walked back to St Columba's for they always preferred to walk when the night was fine.

'It was just *perfect!*' she said, happily.

Years afterwards when she was many miles from her dear Dublin and when she had almost forgotten what a theatre was like, when the zest of life was gone and her heart was sad and old—

often then would Mary Carmichael go back in her dreams to that one evening which somehow seemed to stand out beyond all others in her memory. Many a play had she seen with Dr Delaney, many an evening they had spent together, but none ever seemed to her just so complete—so perfect, as this one when they had sat together in the dear old Gaiety and listened to those words which found an echo in their hearts—'When all was young and fair.'

CHAPTER V

'IN DUBLIN'S FAIR CITY'

Clare Castlemaine was surprised to find how quickly she adapted herself to her new surroundings, and how perfectly at home she soon felt. On their part the Blakes became genuinely fond of their cousin, and each in his or her own particular way did all that was possible to make her new life happy and interesting. Owing to her mourning she could not, of course, join them in their various social pleasures. Nora bemoaned that she could not go to a dance or the theatre, and Shamus spoke of the 'Abbey'—the only place of amusement that his principles would allow him to visit—but he assured her that she would be better able to understand the plays there later on, when she was more used to Irish life. Ursula, however, took her to a few literary lectures, and Bride to social ones, and promised her a typical day's 'slumming' in the near future. Tom accompanied her to one or two recitals of sacred music, and Mr Blake spent an afternoon with her in the National Gallery, and another in the Academy—pictures were his hobby.

Altogether Clare was very glad that she had come to Ireland, although there was much in her present life that puzzled her—and much that gave her 'furiously to think'.

A letter which she wrote to Mrs Webb, after she had been six weeks with the Blakes, expressed some of her doubts, and showed her growing affection for her cousins very clearly.

'DARLING OLD WEBBIE,

I was so pleased to get your letter and to learn that you were feeling stronger, and your cold nearly gone. As for me, I am in robust health! and really I cannot tell you how much better in every way I feel for the change, and how glad I am that I came over here. My cousins grow more delightful every day, and the more I know of them, the more I appreciate them. Oh! Webbie dear, they are *good!* I don't mean in a goody goody sense at all for they never preach but they—*practice* which is far better. Nearly all the family go to seven o'clock Mass every day. Fancy, Webbie, getting up those chilly mornings at 6.30am and going out without a cup of tea or anything! Can you imagine yourself doing it? I really feel quite ashamed when the housemaid brings me my early cup at half-past seven. Breakfast is at 8.30, such a cheery meal—not like the rushing breakfasts I remember at the Wilsons, when father and I stayed there. Like the Blakes, nearly all the family had to go into business every day, and they used to rush down at the last moment, bolt some breakfast, and fly—no time for a civil word to anyone. Here my cousins come in from Mass looking so fresh and happy and gather round the table in such a pleasant homely way. Webbie dear! if there is any good in any religion I am beginning to think it must be in theirs—although it has never been mentioned in my presence. They are most particular in this respect. Not that they hide their religious beliefs or practices. They speak openly amongst themselves in a perfectly plain matter of fact way, and that is what strikes me too—religion is such a definite reality—to them. One would imagine Heaven and its inhabitants to be a sort of next-door neighbour, well known to them all! But they never ask me any questions as to my own religious opinions, and never suggest that I should accompany them to any of their services.

Uncle James is a perfect dear, and they all idolise him, which is no wonder. I see a good deal of him because he and Tom and Mary are generally at home in the evenings, and of course I go out socially very little at present. But we have such pleasant talks, and they are such good company and I hardly miss the others. And then I told you about Angel. If one feels lonely or sad, an hour with this real little angel would dispel one's gloom and make one ashamed to be discontented in her presence. I cannot describe her to you, Webbie; but I am beginning to understand the almost reverential love the others have for her. Bride is going to take me slumming soon—so look out for a letter telling you my adventures on that day. Pat is as great a tease as ever, and Shamus is up to his eyes in Gaelic League work—he says the winter session has commenced. I mentioned this to you before, didn't I?—a sort of society for reviving the old Irish language and customs, and to encourage Irish industries. It seems that Ireland used to have any amount of industries, and manufactures of her own in the past, and the English got them all stopped, as they were interfering with the English trade, and it is only recently they are trying to revive them again, now that better times have come. I think that was awfully unfair, don't you? And I think the English of today must be ashamed of such laws, as we are never taught much Irish history in England, and we don't know how the Irish suffered in the past. It is only in bits and scraps I am picking up my knowledge. Shamus can give date and Act of Parliament for all these laws, but he won't say much before me. Fancy, Webbie, Mary won't use anything in the house that is not of Irish manufacture, if it can be got at all. She says 'Shamus would kill her' if she bought English goods. (That's the way they have of talking—they don't mean anything by it—they say a man is killed dead, and he will only be a little bit hurt.) But the other evening he found a box of English matches on the mantelpiece, and I only wish you could have heard his remarks. He forgot I was in the room—he is always so scrupulously polite for fear he might hurt my English susceptibilities—and I did enjoy listening to him! I had to laugh out at last, and then he saw me and suddenly broke into laughter himself; that's the way with them too, Webbie—but the despised box had gone into the fire. Ursula is going to be a nun—she is to 'enter' as they call it in the spring. I heard them talking about it by chance one day, and oh! Webbie, I could have cried. She is a lovely girl and so clever—she is the musical one of the family and sings—such a voice! It made me feel almost physically sick to think of her buried alive in a convent—and I believe it is a very strict order, where they are up half the night praying, and never get a decent meal. I could not help speaking of this to Mary. 'What a pity,' I said, 'for a girl like Ursula, too! Oh, Mary couldn't you stop her from doing such a foolish thing?' Webbie dear, you should have seen the way she looked at me. I felt quite small when she turned her surprised eyes on me. 'Stop it?' she said. 'Why we consider it an honour, and it makes us so proud of Ursula!'

So you see that is their point of view.

Mary has a great friend—Mary Carmichael—a nurse here in one of the district Homes. She knows London well, as she worked there for some years. She is a convert to the Catholic Church, and I fancy before her conversion she must have enjoyed life in London in a rather frivolous manner. We have had several chats, and she struck me as being a strange mixture. She is an ardent Catholic, and on account of her being a convert, she speaks to me much more freely on religious matters than any of my cousins would ever dream of doing. But Miss Carmichael has all the zeal of the convert, and is not ashamed to show it. On the other hand, she is devoted to the theatre and all other kinds of amusement, and is awfully keen on dancing. Of course I know that from an ordinary Catholic standpoint there is no harm in any of these things in moderation, and when one's duty is not neglected in consequence; but somehow Mary Carmichael always gives me the idea of one that—to use a rather strong expression—would sell her soul for pleasure if she was much tempted, and I fancy too, that if ever any great trouble overtook her, she would not care what she did, or what happened to her. I wonder would she still stick to her religion in that case? I would be curious to know, for I honestly believe nothing else keeps her on the straight path—I suppose some people are built that way. I understand that she is practically engaged to a Dr Delaney—a sort of demigod in Pat's eyes—and as they are apparently devoted to each other, she will probably settle down with him all right. According to the family verdict, he is an epitome of all the virtues and without, not only a single vice, but without even a fault! I have not met this paragon as yet, but he is coming to tea tomorrow with Miss Carmichael, and I confess I am rather anxious to see such a unique specimen of the opposite sex! The only person who does not go into raptures over him is Tom—and somehow I would trust Tom's estimate of a person's character above that of anyone else.

Now, Webbie dear, I have no more news to tell you for this time, so will say good-bye with heaps of love,

from your loving

CLARE.

P.S.—I am becoming quite a housekeeper—on economic lines too, under Mary's supervision. I had no idea how interesting it could be. Mary says I will make an ideal wife for a poor man—but I have to find him first!'

It seemed almost prophetic that the very evening that Clare posted this letter she should meet Anthony Farrell for the first time.

She was sitting in the dining-room alone, reading by the firelight. It was half-past six, and the table was set for seven o'clock tea, but as yet no one was in except Mary, who was upstairs. It was getting dark, but Clare had not yet switched on the light, and as a tall figure entered the room, she barely glanced up from her book, as she remarked, 'Is that you, Tom? The others have not come home yet. Come over to the fire—it's a bit chilly I think.'

The tall figure advanced, but the voice that answered her was not that of her cousin.

'I think you must be Miss Castlemaine. You see I am not Tom! I must ask your forgiveness for coming in like this, but I am always regarded as one of the family, and your cousins are kind enough to allow me the run of the house.'

Clare had risen by this time, and found herself confronting a tall, rather slight young fellow, with dark grey eyes, and hair almost black, so dark it was.

'Oh! I beg your pardon,' she said, 'I thought it was my cousin Tom.'

The intruder smiled.

'May I introduce myself?' he said, 'I am Anthony Farrell, one of Tom's greatest friends—you may have heard your cousin mention my name? I have been away in the country, or you would have had the doubtful pleasure of my acquaintance before this.'

Clare extended her hand in swift friendliness.

'Oh! are you Mr Farrell?' she exclaimed, 'yes, indeed I have often heard Tom, and the others too, speaking of you, and am very glad to meet you.'

'That is very kind of you, Miss Castlemaine,' said Farrell, and taking a seat near her, the two were soon talking away in a quite friendly manner.

Clare had seldom met anyone who interested her so much, and indeed Anthony Farrell was one of those whose personality will always make itself felt. A university man, well-educated, cultured, but not well off, he had entered the ranks of journalism some years ago, and had made rapid strides in that profession. He had travelled a good deal also, and had developed that broad out-look on the world, which your stay-at-home never attains.

He knew London well, and he and Clare were engrossed in the

discussion of a recent play just produced on the London boards, when Mary entered the room, followed by Tom.

Farrell received an enthusiastic welcome from them, and also from Mr Blake and the younger ones, all of whom were shortly gathered round the tea-table.

Conversation was brisk and gay. Anthony, it appeared, had been down in Co Limerick 'doing' some special articles for one of the 'weeklies', for the past two months and he had many questions to ask about mutual friends and interests.

'And how is Mary Carmichael?' he inquired presently. 'Is the affair with Dr Delaney still progressing?'

'Rather!—like a house on fire!' said Pat. 'They go about everywhere together now—theatres, pictures, concerts, and all those National Health Meetings and debates that they are both so keen about.'

'Well! I am very glad to hear it,' said Anthony, 'Delaney is a decent fellow, and I think he deserves Mary Carmichael—and I can't give higher praise to any man, because as you all know, Mary is a very dear and old friend of mine, and I think a lot about her.'

'All the same,' said Pat, 'she is a jolly lucky young woman to have got the right side of Delaney,'—there was a murmur of approval from several, but Clare noticed that Tom Blake was silent. Pat continued, 'Why, I know dozens of girls who would give anything to be in her shoes—and any girl might be proud of her place!'

'Awfully good chap, right enough,' agreed Farrell, adding with a half smile, 'and he certainly will never need a champion to speak for him, Pat, while you have a voice.'

'Oh! Dr Delaney is a sort of demigod to Pat,' said Shamus, 'but to my mind the man might be a little more Irish in his views.'

'Oh! You blessed Gael!' exclaimed Nora, before Pat could answer, 'what on earth do you think Dr Delaney should do? Walk down Grafton street in kilts, I suppose, and look as silly as a lot of Gaelic Leaguers at a Feis?'

'A girl who panders to the Saxon taste in dress, and goes about in hobble skirts and "a glad neck" will hardly appreciate the national costume,' replied Shamus in scathing tones.

But Nora only laughed, and helped herself to more jam.

'We expect Mary and Dr Delaney tomorrow evening, Tony, will you take a look in too?' said Mary, as they were rising from the table.

'If possible, I will,' was the prompt reply, 'I should like to see Mary Carmichael again, and I always enjoy a chat with Delaney.'

On the following evening Clare found herself an interested spectator and an eager listener, as she sat in a corner of the old-fashioned sofa in the Blake's delightful and homely drawing-room. All the family were present, and also Dr Delaney, Mary Carmichael, and Anthony Farrell. Mutual greetings were exchanged—bits of news and harmless gossip about friends and acquaintances followed, and then by degrees all the room settled down to a long conversational evening. Such evenings were quite common amongst them, but Clare found herself listening in genuine amazement as topic after topic of intelligent interest was passed in review and criticism. Everyone had something to say, some remark to make, from Mr Blake in his shabby, but cosy old chair, down to Angel on her comfortable couch near the fire—for this was one of her 'downstairs' nights.

Art, literature, social problems, the stage, the latest concert, the Academy—all were discussed. And then—for what Irish gathering of any kind could refrain from this theme?—the political situation was gone over, and criticised in all its latest aspects.

And here it was that Clare found herself listening with most interest and surprise. For the first time in her life she found herself hearing such things discussed from the Irish point of view—for the first time she heard the Irish ideal of a separate race, separate government, separate nationhood, and she listened in astonishment as English methods and English forms of government were criticised with all that keenness of observation and quickness of perception which is found so highly developed in the Celtic race. Above all she was struck with the fact that these people undoubtedly recognised themselves as a distinct and totally different race from their neighbours across the channel, and to Clare, brought up to consider the Irish as a sort of second-rate English—not quite as civilised or up-to-date as the latter, but capable of improvement under English administration—an aspect of Ireland which, ridiculous as it may appear, is still quite common in the mind of the poor, stolid, John Bull!—for her then to listen to a little genuine Irish criticism was an awakening indeed.

She listened as though in a dream to Mr Blake's quiet logical utterances, to Dr Delaney's slightly sarcastic comments, to Mary Carmichael's eager speech, and to the impassioned tones of

Shamus, with a feeling of bewildered surprise. Her presence was overlooked for the moment. She recognised that very soon, and was content that it should be so. These were her mother's people, her mother's race—and she wanted to learn all she could about them.

'No, Delaney, I don't agree with you and never will!' Shamus was saying, gripping the arm of his chair, and leaning forward in intense earnestness, 'we don't want the Home Rule that the English would offer us! What is it? A shadow—a skeleton of self-government!—only fit for a child to play at! We want complete separation—and by heaven we will get it yet!'

His eyes were blazing, his whole face transformed. Dr Delaney smiled quietly, and the little sarcastic droop of the lips became more noticeable.

'Perhaps—but I doubt it very much,' he said, in his even tones—'as for me, I am no extremist.'

'No extremist!' exclaimed Shamus passionately, 'that means you are lukewarm—tepid—without ideals even! Bah! I'd rather have a red hot Orangeman than one of your milk and water sort!'

There was a ripple of laughter at this, and then Mr Blake took up the argument, touching with quiet, but unerring logic, on some of the flaws of the Bill under discussion.

'I'm afraid this must be all very uninteresting to you?' said a voice beside her, and Clare looked round to see Anthony Farrell seating himself quietly beside her.

'Oh! No!' she cried eagerly, 'on the contrary, I am interested beyond words! I have always wanted to get to know the people of my mother's country—to really know them—and now I have the opportunity.'

He smiled at her with his honest, grey eyes.

'You have indeed,' he said whimsically, 'for—I am afraid to say it!—but for the moment they have forgotten your very existence!'

'Oh! of course—I know that!' she said, adding confidentially, 'That is why I am listening so eagerly, because, as a rule, they are afraid of hurting my feelings or seeming rude, on account of the "English half of me", as Angel expresses it! So I hear very little of their opinions of my father's country, or indeed of their political views at all—so I am most awfully glad to be here now! And it's rather amusing too to think that they are talking away and have forgotten all about the English cousin?' and she laughed in such a whole-hearted girlish way, that Anthony found himself laughing in sympathy.

And so they sat and listened while the talk went on, Anthony putting in a few words of comment or explanation now and then to help her to a better understanding of the topics under discussion.

When at last supper was announced Mary Blake suddenly caught sight of Clare and her companion sitting so quietly together on the sofa.

'Oh, Clare dear!' she cried in repentant accents. 'What will you think of us!—why we quite forgot you, and there we have been talking away without giving you a single thought! Oh! I am sorry!'

But to Mary's surprise her cousin laughed gaily, and more happily than she had done for some time now.

'Well! you see everyone didn't forget me!' she said softly, and she turned her blue eyes towards Anthony.

'So I see,' said Mary smiling, 'Tony you are a dear! and I am so glad you were with Clare—what wretches we all were! But, as she says—everyone didn't forget her!'

Anthony Farrell turned to look at the sweet face beside him.

'It would be hard to forget Miss Castlemaine,' he said quietly.

Clare felt her colour suddenly rising, and then as Mary turned away, she met Tony's eyes as they sought her's. Heart spoke to heart, and from that moment there was no forgetting for either of those two till the end of time.

CHAPTER VI

IN THE SLUMS

What are your thoughts, O! pallid boy—
A dream in a stylish street
With the rain on your rags and gaunt young face,
Where hunger and want have left their trace,
And the mud on your stone-bruised feet?

It was nine o'clock on a foggy November morning, damp and disagreeable like November days often are; and down the Rathmines Road was hastening the usual stream of business and professional people—all going citywards for their day's work. Walking, cycling, or in the trams they hurried along—the lawyer, the clerk, the typist, the shop assistant—men and women, old and young—all hastening to their various avocations. Some of the more prosperous fly by in motors—a penny tram or 'Shank's mare' takes the more humble toiler.

Bride Blake and Clare Castlemaine were walking too, but from choice. It was the morning on which Bride was fulfilling her promise to Clare to take her around that part of the Dublin slums in which she spent so much of her time, and they had started early as Bride had a good many of her 'people' to see.

'I always prefer to walk to my work in the mornings, if you don't mind, Clare,' she said, 'it is really no distance to the Coombe the way I will bring you; but if you would prefer it we will take a tram, as far as it will take us I should say, for there are no trams where I am going this morning.'

'Oh, no, please,' exclaimed Clare, 'I want you just to proceed as if I wasn't with you at all—just do exactly what you would do if you were by yourself.'

'Very well,' said Bride smiling, 'only I stipulate for one condition, Clare, and that is that if you are tired you will tell me at once, because I know that slumming to one who is not accustomed to it, must be very exhausting.'

Clare promised, but she felt so full of interest in what lay before her, that she was sure she would not feel tired at all.

Hitherto she had known only the prosperous and fashionable

parts of the city; she would find her way to Grafton Street and on to O'Connell Street, but north of the 'Pillar' was unknown ground to her, and so also were most of the numerous streets on the south side of the city—especially in the poor neighbourhoods.

The Coombe vicinity offered up an entirely new vista to her, and at first she was half frightened, half repelled, at the dirt and squalor, and the glaring poverty which she now found around her. But Bride passed serenely along as one who was quite familiar with her surroundings—and indeed she was so accustomed to it all that she felt no distaste for even the worst phases of slum life.

'Some of the people look dreadful,' said Clare, half fearfully, as they were subjected to a severe scrutiny from two very dishevelled-looking ladies standing at a rather unsavoury doorway.

Bride laughed.

'They are quite harmless, I assure you!' she said, 'but they don't know you, although they are quite used to me, and they are probably wondering if you rank as a sanitary inspector or health visitor, or a baby club lady, or indeed in what guise you are come to visit them!'

As they turned in the direction of Meath Street she continued:

'Now I am going to take you to some of my favourites, and you will, I think, have a better opinion of this neighbourhood before we finish our morning's work—not that they are all saints,' she added ruefully— 'I will have to let you see a few of my hard cases too!—just for the sake of contrast.'

She pushed open a very shaky door as she spoke and Clare found herself in a dark, evil-smelling hall. The door immediately banged to of its own accord when free of Bride's detaining grasp, and they mounted two flights of very rickety stairs.

Then Bride knocked at a door on her left, and a rather high-pitched voice asked quickly.

'Who's that?'

'It's Miss Blake, James. May I come in?'

'Come in, come in, Miss—and sure you're welcome twice over!' came the answer in the same high-pitched tones—the voice of the blind.

Bride turned the handle and they entered.

Clare found herself in a small but bare and scrupulously clean room; the boards were scrubbed white, and the walls were covered with pictures from the pictorial papers, interspersed here and there with prints of religious subjects. In the window a gold-finch sang his song to a minute patch of blue sky just appearing through the fog, and which he could see from the place where his cage hung.

On a poor but clean bed, covered by a gay patch-work quilt, lay an old man, with white hair and sightless eyes.

'Well, James,' said Bride, taking the thin old hand in her own, 'How are you this morning?'

'Grandly, Miss—grandly, thanks be to God. And how's yourself?'

'I'm very well James, and I have brought a friend to see you to-day.'

'Aye, I heard another step besides your own. And who is it, Miss?'

'It's an English cousin of mine, James.'

'English is it? Ah, well, sure she can't help that same. But maybe now she wouldn't mind letting me hear her speak?'

Feeling rather shy, Clare went over and shook hands, saying a few words of greeting as she did so.

The old face lit up at the sound of her sweet, girlish voice, and he turned his sightless eyes to where he knew that Bride was sitting.

'English or not, Miss Blake, dear,' he said, 'she's the sweet young lady, so she is, and indeed but I'm thinking she has Irish blood in her somewhere.'

Clare laughed then, and spoke more freely.

'My mother was Irish,' she said.

'There now, didn't I know it!' the old man cried in triumph; 'sure I'm never mistaken in anywan's character!'

'Now James,' said Bride, 'I want you to tell my cousin, Miss Castlemaine, something about yourself and how you manage to live. But first of all—are you feeling better these days?'

'Indeed and I am—thanks be to God, and I'm hoping soon to be up and at work again.'

'And what do you work at?' inquired Clare with interest.

'I sells papers, Miss, but it's six weeks now since I was able to be out meself with them. There's a slip of a girleen in the parlour below and she takes them round for me—but, God help us! She's not much good at the job! Of course I have me ould age pension as well, Miss—so I'm wantin' for nothing!'

'But can you live on five shillings a week?' said Clare. To her that seemed an impossible feat.

'Is it live on five shillings a week? Glory be, Miss, and why not?' and even the sightless eyes seemed to express surprise at such a question; 'I make over and above it with the papers, but even without them I'd manage fine. Sure why wouldn't I?'

'Just tell my cousin how you manage, James,' said Bride with a quiet smile.

'Well, Miss, I've one and six for rint, and sixpence a week to the woman below since I've been laid up—she comes to look after me, an' cleans the room, and in the evenings she lights a bit of a fire in the grate beyant, and if I'm able at all I gets up for awhile and sits in the chair—for some of the boys does be comin' in for a chat. Well, I'm not a great ater annyways and a penny roll or a three-ha'penny loaf would do me a good while—and then there's a grain of tay and sugar and a ha'porth of milk every morning. I get a grain of oatmale too, for I take a taste for stirabout these frosty mornings, but a little will do me—and I've a herring now and then and a pig's cheek for Sundays. Miss Blake here got me coal from the Mansion House—the blessin' of God on her!—and the Nurse does let me have a tin of cocoa now and then, and when I was rale bad she got me milk too—may Heaven be her bed!'

'That's Mary Carmichael!' said Bride in a quiet aside, '——this is her district.'

But Clare was looking at the old man, so happy and 'contented with little' indeed!

'I don't smoke, Miss, and I don't snuff,' he was saying 'so that saves me a lot. But I do enjoy a good cup of tay—but sure it's only tay dust that they do be sellin' in the hucksters' shops around here.'

'I'll send you some really good tea, James,' Clare cried eagerly, 'you will take it as a little present from me, won't you? even though I am English,' she added half laughingly.

'Take it, Miss? and why not? Sure I'll take it and pray for you every living night! As to being English, sure as I said before you can't help that, and after all it's only half English yez are annyways. Talkin' of tay,' he went on after a moment, 'do yez know how many cups of tay the great Dr Johnson used to drink?'

'No,' said Clare, smiling, 'five or six perhaps?'

The old man laughed heartily.

'Five or six is it?' he echoed, 'no, but twenty-five and that at wan sitting, mind yez! Twenty-five cups of tay at wan sitting!'

And he was still chucking to himself over this, one of his favourite yarns, when the two girls were descending the shaky stairs on their way to the street once more.

'Oh! Bride!' cried Clare, 'the poor old man! And he seems so contented too! Oh! how does he manage to exist at all.'

'Well! he told you how,' said Bride smiling quietly 'and he really is happy Clare, and a perfect saint—always the same happy, thankful old soul. He is a lesson in contentment for all of us—and here is another!' as she entered a doorway a little further down the street.

A little 'return room' up two flights of stairs—stairs so dark that Clare found herself stumbling and groping at every step until Bride after a gentle knock opened the room door and they entered.

Bare and clean too—as clean as old James O'Brien's, but with a difference that one saw at a glance that *this* was a woman's room. Poor as it was there were still to be seen the many little touches that proclaimed a woman's hand. A few geraniums—sickly enough looking but still making a brave struggle for existence—were on the window sill; a gaily coloured cushion brightened up a shabby old armchair, and in a corner of the room stood a little altar, cheaply but tastefully decorated. Religious pictures adorned the walls for the most part, but side by side with the 'Holy Family' or the cheap prints of the Madonna and Child, would be found fashion plates of ladies with impossible figures compressed into impossible gowns. A small—very small—fire burned in the tiny grate, and on a low stool before it crouched a pale, emaciated young woman, whose racking cough had been heard as they were ascending the stairs.

'Well, Mary,' said Bride, 'how are you today? I hope you feel a little better—no don't get up please. I have brought a cousin of mine—Miss Castlemaine—to see you.'

The sick woman smiled, and held out a skeleton hand. 'You are welcome Miss,' she said to Clare, who was regarding her with compassionate eyes, 'won't you sit down please? You will find a chair over there.'

Mary Duffy was far advanced in consumption and lived with her sister in this one little room. The sister earned six shillings a week and her food by doing daily work from eight in the morning until eight at night, at a large house in the suburbs. Mary had not been working for many a day, so that she had no state insurance to draw and all the two women had to rely upon was the sister's pittance, of which two shilling went for rent and at least a shilling or one and six for fire and light.

'But, of course me sister gets her dinner and tea where she works, Miss, and often Mrs Browne sends me out a tasty bit now and then to tempt me, for it's not much I can eat, and Nurse Carmichael and Miss Blake here do be very good to me with milk and cocoa, and last week we got the coal from the Mansion House, and God only knows the relief it was to us, for it does be bitter cold these nights, and I'm thinkin' that I must have no blood at all left in me body—I do be shivering half the day these times!'

'And how is Maggie?' asked Bride.

Maggie was the sister, a delicate girl too, and Mary Carmichael had told Bride that she was afraid she would contract the disease from the other. Sharing not only the same room but even the same bed, underfed and overworked, and her sister in such an advanced stage that she was really dangerous to others—could poor Maggie escape? Mary Carmichael who lived so to speak in the sorrows and joys of her patients, often worried over this case.

'Well, now Miss, she's grand—thanks be to God! Although she does be bet out altogether at night. And these few mornings I was wanting her to take a cup of tea and a cut of bread before she went out—but no, she wouldn't.'

Bride Blake, who knew the reason, said nothing; but Clare asked:

'But why wouldn't she—did she feel sick?'

'Oh, no, Miss, but you see Maggie is a real good girl and receives every morning, but she doesn't have time to come back here for a cup of tea after seven o'clock Mass, because she has to be at Terenure sharp to the minute of eight, and it takes her every minute of the time to walk there.'

Clare listened open-eyed—all this was beyond her.

'Oh!' was all she could say in astonishment, adding, 'well, I hope she gets a real good breakfast when she gets there—for she would want it.'

'Oh! yes Miss, she manages a cup of tea and a slice of bread, except of course they are very busy or the like—and it's a terrible busy house—and then it might be eleven or twelve o'clock before she could break her fast.'

Clare was speechless from bewilderment, as the woman noticed with some surprise.

'But sure she doesn't mind, Miss,' she said cheerfully, 'Maggie wouldn't miss going to the Altar for anything—not if it was to cost her life itself.'

At this moment a quick, light footstep sounded on the stairs, followed by a business-like rap at the door, and the next instant Mary Carmichael in her nurses' uniform stood before them. Her face lit up with pleasure as she saw her two friends, but even while she was greeting them her eyes were scanning the room with professional observation.

'I think this window will open a little more,' she remarked, and as she spoke she was pushing up the crazy window and deftly keeping it in place with a wooden peg.

'I have got the camp bed for you at last Mary,' she said then, 'it will be sent to you this evening—bed clothes and all.'

'Oh! Nurse, *thank* you!' and the sick woman's eyes lit up. 'Oh! I am grateful for it—and not for myself Nurse dear as you know well, but I'm fretting this long while for fear harm would come to Maggie through her sleeping with me. May God bless you, Nurse!'

Mary Carmichael's eyes were strangely tender as she smiled down on the poor creature. Her patients always saw the best side of Mary and loved her accordingly. She turned now in a half-teasing way to Clare.

'Well! Are *you* suffering from the slumming craze too?' said she; 'it's becoming so fashionable just now amongst 'the quality' that really we poor workers may soon take a back seat.'

'Ah! Mary, you know better!' said Bride, 'I only wish that I could get at the heart of my people like you do.'

'Would you like to finish the morning with me?' said Mary, 'I have a few places to go to yet that I think will open Miss Castlemaine's eyes. After all when she *is* slumming she may as well do the thing properly, and I observe,' she added, as after saying good-bye to Mary Duffy they were again on their way, 'that you are only showing her your pet cases, Bride. Now I will bring Miss Castlemaine to a few 'real hard cases' for a change. But I think that you had better go on with your own visits and meet us at half past twelve in St Patrick's Park and we will then go and have a cup of tea somewhere—Miss Castlemaine will need it by then I expect.'

'Well! Yes, I think she will if *you* are going to take her round! But that will be the best Mary, because you will be able to show her far more of the real slums than I can—although I know them fairly well—but your footing amongst them is so altogether different—they have always a good word for the nurse, somehow!'

So they separated—Bride going her own way—and Clare

presently found herself walking by Mary Carmichael's side along one of the worst alleys in that locality.

Slovenly women and dirty ragged children sprawled on the pavements, starved dogs and mangy cats prowled around in the gutter in search of food, while evil smells seemed to arise from everywhere and choke her.

But she noticed that the looks directed towards her present escort were very different from those to which she and Bride had been subjected. Evidently 'the nurse' was well known, and both liked and respected by these denizens of the slums.

'They look very bad,' said Mary quietly, as they passed swiftly along, 'but they really are not half as bad as they appear—although some of them are bad enough, Heaven knows! as you will see before long. Just come in here now!'

They entered a low doorway, and passing through an indescribably dirty entrance—hall it could hardly be designated—went down two flights of filthy stairs, Mary calling back to Clare to hold her skirts well off the ground, and found themselves looking in through the open door of an under-ground kitchen.

To Clare the place seemed full of unwashed humanity—the nauseating smell of which met her on the threshold with such force that it seemed a solid wall of bad gases, and she had to brace herself to go forward and advance by Mary's side further into the room—if room it could be called.

It was one of the usual damp underground kitchens of the slums, with one tiny window opening on to a back yard, the smell from which—when Mary, as in duty bound had opened it, was little if any better than that of the fetid kitchen itself.

A young woman, down at heel, ragged and drink-sodden, was sitting nursing a tiny unwashed morsel of a baby; three other small children were sitting on the dirty damp floor; a boy of about sixteen—an embyro criminal in appearance—lounged against the one rickety table smoking a fag; a girl a year or so older, her hair in 'curlers', and nearly as dirty and down at heel as the woman—but still with a certain attempt at tawdry finery—was sitting reading a novelette, a man lay on a filthy 'bed' in the corner snoring loudly, and evidently sleeping off the previous night's debauch; and an old hag sat in the chimney corner smoking a short clay pipe.

This last was the patient, and Mary Carmichael rapidly turned up her sleeves, and opening her bag took from it some clean paper which she spread on the table and then arranged her dressings. The woman, still holding the baby on one arm produced a none too clean basin which Mary rinsed several times from the kettle before proceeding to use it for cleaning the old woman's ulcerated leg. She spoke little but deftly and swiftly finished the dressing, washed her hands, repacked her bag, and was ready for the next case.

But short as the time was it seemed infinitely too long to poor Clare, standing in embarrassed silence near the door—holding Mary's cloak which the latter had handed to her in thankfulness that she could do so, and not have to deposit it anywhere in the room.

Clare had never seen such a scene of dirt and squalor before—but she was almost afraid to look around, for she felt the bold, insolent gaze of the girl, the keen scrutiny of the young hooligan, and the furtive looks which the woman threw her now and then from her bleary eyes. Simply as Clare was dressed, there was a look of distinction and style about her, which was not lost upon those beings of the underworld who were used to living by their wits, and who possessed that quick perception and keenness of observation which is so noticeable amongst the Dublin poor.

But now Mary had finished, and taking her cloak from Clare she slipped it on.

'Now mind what I'm telling you, Granny,' she remarked, as she prepared to depart, 'if you don't give up the porter that leg of yours will never heal!'

And taking no notice of the old lady's asseverations that she 'didn't know the taste of it!' Mary accompanied Clare up the filthy stairs and out into the street once more.

The latter drew in a breath of the cold air, as she said in accents of relief.

'Oh! Miss Carmichael! I am so glad to be out of that place! What awful people! And so dirty. But I suppose they are very poor?'

'Not so poor as you think,' said Mary quietly, 'they are of the class that will always manage to live from hand to mouth someway or other. There is, probably, not a charitable organisation in the city of any denomination which they don't know, and of which they don't make use from time to time. The man too, can earn good wages on the quays when he likes, but he drinks it nearly all. The old woman has the old age pension, the boy sells papers, and the girl—well, I am afraid she is not all she ought to be. But here we are at my next case—and I think you will like this better!'

They entered the 'top front' of a house overlooking Patrick's Park. It was an untidy but not dirty room, the walls of which, in the usual tenement style, were pasted over with all sorts of pictures. The table was littered with the remains of some meal—probably breakfast; the two windows were open, and on an improvised bed drawn up close to one of them was a little deformed boy of about seven years. Two bright intelligent eyes shone out from the pale wizened face—and how that face lit up as Mary entered the room.

'Well, Jimmy,' she said, with a smile, 'and how are you today?'

'I'm grand, Nurse, thank you. Me mother is at the market, but she left the kettle on, and the basin and the cold water are there beyant.'

A bad tubercular abscess of the hip had to be dressed here, and as she went about her work Mary gave Clare an outline of the case. The mother was a widow with five other children, all of school age. She was a fish dealer and generally had to be out at the markets very early; the other children gave Jimmy his breakfast, and settled him for the day as well as they could before they went off to school, but after that he was alone till their return, save for the ministrations of the kind neighbour who lived on the same landing—in the 'top back'. Even as she spoke the door opened quietly, and an old woman came slowly into the room.

'Is the Nurse here, Jimmy?' she asked, and Clare looking closely at her, noticed that she was looking before her with the unseeing eyes of the blind.

'Yes, Mrs Keogh, ma'am, she is, and another lady with her.'

'I was thinkin' I heard another footstep,' said the blind woman, 'have you all you want Nurse?'

'Yes, everything, thank you, Mrs Keogh,' said Mary, and after a few minutes the old woman went out as quietly as she had come in.

'She is living on the Old Age pension,' said Mary, and she fastened her bandage with skilful fingers, 'and is very good to Jimmy here when he is all alone. Isn't she Jimmy?'

'She is, Miss,' with a soft shy smile—a smile which grew bigger and brighter as Mary produced an apple and some chocolate from one of her many pockets.

As they went downstairs she said softly to Clare, 'That is one of my child martyrs; I have several others as well.'

Clare's eyes were full of tears and for the moment she could not speak, but many a visit she paid to Jimmy that winter, and many a toy and more substantial comforts also found their way into the poor fish hawker's room.

They saw several other cases, and then it was time to meet Bride for the promised cup of tea. A short walk brought them all into the more prosperous streets, and seated in the pretty tea-room, the two workers were soon enjoying their tea and cakes and chatting away to their heart's content.

But Clare was silent and very quiet. She was totally unused to such sights as those to which she had been brought that morning. They had made a deep impression on her, and she found herself quite unable to shake off a feeling of gloom and depression.

To Mary Carmichael and Bride Blake of course it was simply part of their day's work, and they were too thoroughly used to such scenes and too well accustomed to slum life—both good and bad—to be in anyway affected by it.

'We did not even show you the worst phases of it,' said Bride, as she poured herself out another cup of tea, 'the real vice and degradation of some of the people is just as awful in its way as the real unselfish goodness of others is wonderful!'

Mary Carmichael nodded.

'Yes, I know what you mean,' she said quietly, 'I remember someone once asking me what conditions of life I really found in the slums, and I answered that I found there the very worst and the very best of human nature.'

CHAPTER VII

'THE LIGHT THAT NEVER WAS ON SEA OR LAND!'

Mary Carmichael was buttoning her tweed coat and settling her little fur cap becomingly on her wavy hair. Supper at St Columba's was just over, and she was going out for a while with Nurse Seeley.

It was the last week of November and the nights were clear and frosty, and from her window high up at the top of the great house, Mary could see the street lamps shining on the frosty pavements. She threw her fur over her shoulder, and took her muff in her hands just as Nurse Seeley, after a little knock, entered the room.

'Ready, Mac?' she cried, 'Come along, there's an old dear—it's nearly nine o'clock.'

Nurse Seeley was going to one of the evening dispensaries in the city to report to the doctor there about a rather bad case of his which she was nursing in her district—and incidentally to have a talk with him on other matters as well, for he was a great friend of hers—and was keenly interested also in Mary Carmichael for reasons of his own. The two girls descended the long flights of stairs, and were soon walking briskly down the square and into the broad streets beyond. These were presently left behind and in a very short time they were standing at the corner of a slum street on the north side of the city—one of those streets of large houses with great entrance halls and wide staircases, where in Georgian times ladies were wont to descend from sedan chairs with link boys in attendance. There are drawing-rooms in these houses—and often a fine carved mantelpiece may be found there still intact—which were the scenes of many a dance and many a gay party in days long gone by. In those same rooms now are whole families living together as best they can—some in cleanliness and decency, others again sunk in drink and degradation.

'St Paul's Dispensary' is at the corner of one such street, and the light is shining through the drawn blinds.

'He's not away yet, anyhow,' said Nurse Seeley, 'we will ring the bell.'

Their ring was answered by a tall female in rusty black and smelling of snuff. This was Miss Becket who cleaned the surgery and generally 'looked after' the place during Dr Head's absence.

'Oh, good evening, Miss Becket,' said Nurse Seeley, 'is the doctor in?'

'He is, Miss—come in please. The last patient has just gone in and so he will be disengaged now in a few moments.'

'And how are you, Miss Becket?' asked Mary Carmichael, as they entered the small waiting-room with its gas stove, couple of chairs, and benches round the wall.

'Well, now, I can't say that I am well Miss—for I am not. I do get a terrible pain in me back and chest—but, of course, I mustn't complain. We have been very busy lately.' Miss Becket always spoke of the doctor and herself as 'we'—'and it has been terribly late at night before we got finished sometimes. Still, as I said before, it's no use complaining.'

'Not a bit, Miss Becket,' said Nurse Seeley, smiling, while Mary listened in quiet amusement—she always enjoyed Miss Becket's views on life and things in general.

'And how are you, Miss?' that lady now enquired turning to her, 'you have not been to see us lately—I hope you have been well?'

'Oh, quite, thank you, Miss Becket,' replied Mary, 'but like yourself I have been very busy.'

'Ah, well, don't overdo it now—take care of yourself in time and mind your own health. How often I said those same words to me poor brother—taking a good pinch of snuff— but dear me, he never minded what I said—not till it was too late!'

The two girls said nothing. They both knew the whole history of her brother's life, illness, and death, but once Miss Becket got started on that theme, there was no turning her as they knew to their cost.

'As he said to me the very night before he was taken—"Martha," sez he, "You've been a good sister to me, and if I had only minded half of what you said to me, I——" '

At this juncture, to the great relief of her hearers, the surgery door opened, there were voices in the hall as the last patient was shown out, and the next moment Dr Head was shaking hands with them, and ushering them into his cosy little surgery.

Maurice Head was about forty years of age, short, clean-shaven and decidedly inclined to embonpoint. He liked the creature comforts of life and enjoyed a good dinner, or a good joke almost equally well—for he was full of a genial *bonhomie* which endeared him to many. He was married, and knew what trouble was, but he was devoted to his children, and they were one of the bright spots in his life.

He wheeled two chairs up to the gas fire now, and fussed round his visitors, making them comfortable. He was delighted they had called round, for he enjoyed an evening like this—free *pro tem.* from 'the wife's' supervision—as keenly as a schoolboy on holiday.

'You may go, Miss Becket,' he called out, 'I'll put out the lights before I leave. Now, then—you two—how's the world using you, and how is St Columba's?'

'Oh, just the same old six and eightpence,' said Nurse Seeley, laughing. 'What would you expect? I would have been here sooner only for Miss Carmichael here—I had to wait for her to put on her best bib and tucker!'

Dr Head leaned back, and surveyed Mary with a critical eye.

'Well, I must say the result is very becoming,' he announced, adding, 'I'm only sorry Delaney won't be here tonight.'

Mary Carmichael said nothing, but the red flag mounted to her cheeks, and Nurse Seeley laughed.

'Don't tease her, Doctor,' she said, 'she pretends to be so shy—she and Dr Delaney are just friends, you know—nothing more.'

'Gad! I never met such a pair in my life,' said the doctor, and giving his shoulders a characteristic shrug, he suddenly turned and looked Mary squarely in the face.

'Look here, my lady,' he asked then—'*do* you, or do you not care for Delaney?'

The girl was so taken by surprise that she could not answer—she simply sat and looked at him.

'You know,' he went on, 'I look upon Delaney as my best friend—there is no man on this earth for whom I have a greater regard. He is a man in a thousand—aye in a million—and you know it! Now do you care for him or not?'

'Oh, Dr Head!' was all she could breath; then as he still looked steadily at her she murmured, 'of course as a friend there is no one I think more of, but I am sure—*quite* sure that *he* regards *me* in no other light.'

And indeed so she had been thinking lately. Matters had progressed no further between herself and Dr Delaney. They went everywhere together, they talked as intimately and as confidentially as ever, they were in fact as chummy as they had ever been—but beyond that he never went. And so Mary was beginning to think that it was only friendship after all that he felt for her.

'Ah! what nonsense are you talking?' exclaimed Dr Head. *Friendship*!—queer friendship when a man can talk of nothing but one girl all the time—enjoy nothing if she is not with him—yarns by the hour about her manifold perfections—and so on. Friendship where are you—now do you care for him or not?'

Mary flushed again, but this time she raised her eyes, and looked her questioner straight in the face.

'And if I did, why should I tell you?' she asked proudly. But Dr Head leant forward and placed his hand on hers. 'Because I want to see him happy—that's why,' he said quietly, and the bantering tones left his voice and he went on, 'he's a man that could be happy with a good woman—and I know you are that—and he wants someone to liven him up, for you know how often he gets melancholy and downhearted—all about nothing. His digs are comfortable enough but after all they're only digs, and Delaney is the type of man who would enjoy home life. The worst of it is he is so decidedly shy and reserved. Come now! Why don't you help him? Do you ever give him a bit of encouragement at all?'

Mary said nothing, but Nurse Seeley interposed. 'Encouragement, indeed she doesn't, Doctor. Why she often snubs the poor fellow for nothing, and is as cold as an iceberg when he's near!'

'There you are now,' he cried, 'and you should just put your arms around his neck and tell him that you love him!'

'Oh! Dr Head,' Mary cried, aghast, and Nurse Seeley broke into a peal of laughter at the sight of her face. 'Well, do as you like now,' said Maurice Head, 'I've given you good sound advice, and I know what I'm talking about. But Heaven knows the pair of you would try anyone's patience. As much in love with each other as two mortals can be, and yet neither of you will advance an inch out of your shell! Well, I've said my say and can do no more,' and with another characteristic shrug of his plump shoulders the doctor turned the conversation. However, later on when he was parting with them at the corner of the square in which was St Columba's Home, he gave Mary's hand an extra pressure, with the words, 'Sleep on my advice, now! Good night!'

But there was little sleep for Mary Carmichael that night. Dr Head's words had sunk deeply into her mind and she could not forget them. Not indeed that she wanted to forget them—far from it. The very thoughts and hopes which they conjured before her were inexpressibly sweet to her. Could Theodore Delaney really care for her? Dr Head should know—the pair were inseparable chums and Mary knew that Dr Delaney must have spoken pretty freely to the other man before he would speak as he had spoken to her that night. But still—could it be possible? Could life hold such happiness for her, happiness so great, so incomparable, that she was afraid even to let her thoughts dwell on it.

If only she knew his feelings towards her—knew them for certain. But she realised that for her to encourage him in any way or to make the slightest advance would be impossible. She simply could not do such a thing. Mary was intensely proud—proud to a fault—and the bare idea of letting any man see that she cared for him without first knowing for certain that he loved her was simply out of the question and yet—if he really cared and was only holding back after all through reserve or uncertainty as to her feeling—in that case should she not encourage him a little? He was as proud as herself and very reticent, and disliked to display much emotion or feeling at any time—an intensely sensitive man in every way. She knew all this, but still she shrank involuntarily at the very thought of letting him get a glimpse of her feelings. Let him but speak and tell her that which she was hungering to hear and she was ready to pour forth the love of her heart to him without shame or reserve. But that she should make the first advance—no, the thing was simply not possible to her.

'But I wish I knew—oh! I wish I knew!' she said over and over again as she tossed about in useless efforts to settle to sleep.

Then a sudden thought struck her. She would start a Novena for the Feast of the Immaculate Conception on December 8th, and leave everything in Our Lady's hands.

'It's all I can do!' she thought. 'Our Lady will help me—she never failed me yet! I will not bother one bit more myself, but start the Novena in the morning—it's the 29th, and then I will leave everything to her.'

And so, feeling more at peace, Mary dipped her finger into the little font of holy water beside her bed, and making the sign of her redemption with a sigh of relief, she composed herself at last to sleep.

A few evenings after this she was visiting the Blakes. Mary Blake met her in the hall and took her upstairs to her own special sanctum for a little chat before they joined the others. The 'two Marys' were inseparable friends and really attached to each other.

'Well, dearie, and how is the world using you? And are working away, thinking of everyone except yourself, as usual?' asked Mary Carmichael, as she drew out her hatpins, and stood for a moment arranging her hair before the mirror.

Miss Blake laughed.

'Yes, I'm just as usual,' she said, 'it's all very well to talk my dear, but if I didn't look after the house and the inhabitants thereof, I wonder who would?'

'All the same,' replied the other, 'you spoil them Mary—however, I don't suppose you would be happy if you hadn't them to spoil! And how is the English cousin getting on ?' 'Oh, grand,' was the reply, 'and do you know, Mary, I am certain that Anthony Farrell is really in love with her, and I believe she likes him, too—only she is so cold and quiet, it's hard to tell how she feels.'

'Really!' cried the other, turning round with quick interest, 'how charming! Anthony is such a good fellow and I took a great fancy to your cousin from the first moment I saw her.'

'Yes, she is a dear girl,' said Mary Blake.Then coming near to her friend she put her hands on her shoulders and looked at her lovingly—earnestly.

'And what about yourself, dearie?' she said.

Mary Carmichael flushed quickly and then paled again.

'Oh! I—I don't know, Mary,' she answered almost in a whisper, 'sometimes I think that he cares, and sometimes I—well I just begin to think that it would be too good to be true.'

Mary Blake had always been the other's greatest confidant and so now half reluctantly and half gladly she told her what Dr Head had said, and also about the Novena for the Feast of the Immaculate Conception—now almost half-way through.

Mary Blake kissed her fondly.

'You did right dear,' she said softly, 'to take all your troubles and perplexities to the Blessed Mother—you may be sure that she will make everything right for you. But come now—we must go down, or they will be waiting tea for us.'

As they emerged into the corridor Clare Castlemaine was passing on her way downstairs too, and greeted Miss Carmichael in her usual quiet way, but her eyes showed that she was really glad to meet her again.

'Well, Miss Castlemaine,' said Mary, smiling, 'have you quite recovered from your slumming experiences yet?' Clare smiled back, but her face was grave as she replied:

'I have not forgotten it, anyhow!'

'Don't think too much about it' advised the other. 'I'm beginning to think that it was rather a mistake to bring you into such surroundings at all. One needs to be thoroughly accustomed to such scenes before one can face them unmoved. Of course Bride and myself are immune, so to speak.'

They reached the dining-room as they spoke, from which came a buzz of talk and laughter. As Clare advanced she was suddenly conscious that the voices were all speaking in an unknown tongue—unknown at least to her, for she could not understand one word.

Clare had been for years in France and spoke French perfectly, and German fairly well, and had a smattering of Italian—but she found herself wondering what this language could be, as she stood for a few moments, taking stock, as it were, of the people in the room. Mary had told her that some friends were coming to see Shamus, but that was all she knew. She looked at them curiously now as they called out greetings to her cousin and Mary Carmichael—still in that strange, unknown tongue.

Shamus was there, sitting beside a small, dark girl in a plain 'tailor-made' coat of Donegal tweed, with a red Tam o' Shanter on her rather unruly curls, and Clare noticed at once that these two seemed very interested in each other. Anthony Farrell was standing talking to a tall, clean shaven, very clever-looking man of about thirty-five to forty; and a slight, fair-haired girl wearing a pince-nez, stood near them and joined in the conversation rather languidly. The rest of the Blake family were scattered through the room here and there. As Clare advanced, her cousin Mary slipped an arm round her and drew her towards the group round the fire.

'Now please—you Gaels!' she called out, 'return to the hated Saxon tongue!—my cousin does not understand Irish! Clare, this is Norah Donovan,' as the red Tam o' Shanter came forward, 'and this is Eithne Malone'—indicating the languid lady, 'and this—last—but not least—is Mr Robert Hewson—and they are all Irish mad like Shamus.'

A peal of good-natured laughter answered her and a few remarks in Gaelic were hurled at her, but just then Mr Blake came in and tea was commenced—the conversation, in deference to Clare and a few of the others who 'hadn't the Gaelic' being carried on in English.

After tea Clare found herself sitting by Anthony Farrell, and as usual they had plenty to say to each other. Somehow when they were together, their surroundings were forgotten and in a few minutes they would be deep in conversation, discussing a hundred and one things of interest to both. They had become such real friends that Clare took his ready sympathy—it was almost intuition where she was concerned—almost as a matter of course, and to-night she discussed with him—not for the first time—those pitiful conditions of life which had been revealed to her during her one, never to be forgotten, morning in the slums.

'It seems so *unjust*!' she was saying now. 'Why have these poor people to suffer like that? In some cases I know it is largely their own fault—but not in all. And then the poor children—oh! if you had but seen the little suffering atom that Miss Carmichael was visiting—poor wee thing, and all alone as one might say, for the whole day. Oh! it was pitiful!'

Anthony Farrell smiled down at her.

'I have seen such cases—many of them,' he said sadly, 'I did a number of special articles last year, on slum life, for a Christmas copy, and well—I'm pretty hardened for I've knocked about a bit in my time, but still, as you say, the *kiddies*—and, well—I felt jolly bad for some time after.'

'And yet you are a Christian!' said Clare. There was no sneer in her voice, no contempt, but just a great note of wonder and surprise, as if she was stating something that was incomprehensible to her, and as she spoke her clear, blue eyes looked straight into his.

Farrell returned her gaze unflinchingly, but his eyes were pitiful as he looked at her.

'Yes,' he answered quietly, 'I am—thank God—a Christian.'

'You are even a Catholic,' continued Clare, 'and that church seems to me to be the most uncompromising of all the different forms of Christianity. Of course I know there are Christians and Christians—I knew various sorts and sects in London, and the latitude which they allowed themselves in the matter of doctrine was very great. It seemed to me that one could believe or disbelieve almost anything and yet *call* oneself a Christian. But since I came to live with my cousins I have begun to see that the Catholic faith is very different. It may be right or wrong—I don't know—but to its followers it is certainly a *living* faith—a faith that can say this is wrong or that is right—you may do this, you may not do that—a faith that can speak with authority—an authority that will be obeyed without question of argument.'

Anthony Farrell's pale features lit up.

'You are right, Miss Castlemaine,' he said, 'ours is the living faith—and we know it!'

Clare sighed, and looked at him wistfully.

'It must be a great, an unspeakable comfort to you,' she said, 'your faith. I would give almost anything to feel like that—to have *some* belief in *something.* A woman without religion of some sort is never happy!'

Anthony smiled—a trifle sadly.

'Well for my part,' he answered, 'I think that any human soul—let it be man or woman—who is living or existing, perhaps I should say—devoid of any spiritual help, must be wretched beyond words.'

He hesitated a moment, glancing at the pale, grave face of the girl beside him and noticing the restless look in her eyes, and his voice faltered a little as he went on, 'but you, surely if you wished—your cousins—'

But she stopped him with a quick movement—lifting her hands in protest.

'No, no!' she said, 'it's no good—no good! My poor father thought he was doing it all for the best—and anyway he only acted on principle—when he would not allow any religious training to be included in my education.

'When I was eighteen he allowed me to read, study any books on any form of religious belief that I liked, but I simply got so frightfully muddled that I gave it all up in despair. It is only lately—since I came here and have seen what religion—real religion—can mean to people, that I have got restless again. But don't let us talk of these things any more. Tell me,' with a quick change of tone, 'who are these people—these friends of my cousin Shamus? I have not met them before.'

Anthony smiled as he glanced across the room to the group of enthusiastic Gaelic Leaguers, now gathered once more together and discussing earnestly some knotty point in connection with the Irish language movement.

'Well, to begin,' he said, 'we will start with Norah Donovan. She is a school teacher and lives with her people in Harold's Cross direction. She is very clever—has any amount of letters after her name—and is a hard worker. After her day at school she devotes most of her evenings to the study of Irish, attending Irish Classes and lectures, and giving a helping hand to others. She is young and enthusiastic, a great dancer—Irish dances of course!—sings very well. In fact, she is full of life and happiness, with a spice of mischief in her composition, and I rather fancy that your cousin Shamus is her devoted slave. Well! now that finishes number one on the list!'

Clare laughed and he continued.

'Number two—Eithne Malone. Music is her speciality, particularly the old Irish music, and she has taken gold medals and heaven knows what besides, at nearly every Feis in the country. She is a hot Sinn Féiner, and speaks at all their meetings and so on—only that you happen to be half a Celt I doubt if she would have shaken hands with you. She looks lazy and languid, doesn't she? That's all a pose. You should see her when she is aroused—pouring forth one of her speeches—you wouldn't know her.'

Clare was still looking at the lady in question when Anthony went on to speak of the third stranger.

'And now there's Robert Hewson for you. A North of Ireland Presbyterian—and an out-and-out Home Ruler. His ancestors fought with Henry Joy McCracken "in the days of yore," and the family have always been good Irishmen down to the present time.'

Clare looked her surprise as she said:

'But I thought that the North——'

'That they were all Orangemen, easy dupes of mercenary leaders?' said Farrell. 'Well, unfortunately, that answers for a large percentage of them at the present day, but they are not all like that. Ah, no, not at all. Why, in '98, some of the leaders of the movement were northerners, and also Protestants. And what was Robert Emmet and Lord Edward Fitzgerald, and dozens of others—all good Protestants, and all gave their lives for Ireland. As far as religion goes it just happens that Catholicity is the religion of the majority in this country—in spite of every possible effort on

England's part to make it otherwise—but we won't touch on the Penal days now—and so most Irishmen are Catholic—but many a Protestant has been a better Irishman than his Catholic fellow-countryman.'

'Well these are new thoughts for me!' said Clare, 'I am certainly seeing things in a different aspect since I came to my mother's country. And is that really Irish that they are speaking? And can you speak it also?'

'Yes, that is really Irish—or the Gaelic as we prefer to call it—and I can speak it a little, but not with the fluent ease of our friends over here. You see they are nearly always at it, and especially in the winter they have any amount of Gaelic Classes going—but I haven't the time to study it as I should wish.'

'It sounds very strange to my ears,' said Clare, 'is it difficult to learn?'

'Well—yes, I think so—rather. But some way it has such fascination for one that its difficulties are soon overcome. It is a very ancient tongue, you know, probably one of the oldest in the world—and don't think me rude if I remind you that it was a spoken language and a language in which poems were written and battle and love songs sung, centuries before the mongrel accumulation of words—gathered from other languages and called English—was ever known.'

Clare smiled and then laughed, although for a moment the 'English half' of her had felt rather vexed.

'Oh, please, don't apologise,' she cried, 'I can assure you that I am rapidly finding my level since I came to Ireland.'

Anthony was about to answer her, but just then several of the visitors came over to day good-night, and conversation became general so that he had not an opportunity of any further talk with Clare.

'The two Marys'—as the Blake family called them, said good-bye in the hall, and Mary Blake whispered into her friend's ear as she helped her on with her coat—'you will let me know the result of your Novena, won't you dear?'

And Mary Carmichael with one of her vivid blushes, nodded her head, but said nothing.

She was thinking of Mary Blake's words a few evenings later on the 7th December—as accompanied by Nurse Seeley she rang the bell of St Paul's Dispensary, and was ushered into the waiting-room by the polite Miss Becket.

'The last patient is with the doctor now,' she informed them, 'and I know you ladies will excuse me if I leave you as I promised to call and see a sick friend tonight, and I don't like to be too late—it's after nine as it is. Sit down and warm yourselves at the stove—the Doctor won't be long, I'm sure,' and so saying, with a jerk at her rusty bonnet string, she departed.

The minutes went by but still the last patient lingered. The two girls were chatting over their day's work and discussing an especially interesting case, when suddenly three sharp little rings—a signal evidently—came to the outer door.

Mary Carmichael flushed and then paled a little, and Nurse Seeley laughed.

'There's dear Theodore!' she said, 'will you open the door Mac?' but Mary only smiled and shook her head, shrinking back a little as she did so. She was highly strung this evening, and in spite of all her efforts to be calm and collected she felt that she was in an acutely nervous condition. She was standing at the further end of the waiting-room when Dr Delaney followed Nurse Seeley in, and their eyes met across the room in one lightning glance, and Mary felt her heart give a great throb and then rush madly on for a few minutes.

They shook hands and the three seated themselves, Dr Delaney starting to talk and joke—a lot of nonsense most of it, but it served the purpose of putting Mary at her ease, and soon she was talking and laughing away as usual.

Dr Head found quite a merry group, when he entered presently, after having at length got rid of a rather garrulous patient. He suggested a move into the surgery as being more comfortable—it contained a few easy chairs, and was larger and more convenient in every way than the little waiting-room with its benches and hard chairs.

The two girls rose and Nurse Seeley followed Dr Head from the room, but Dr Delaney remained seated and as Mary passed him to follow the others, he put out a hand and laid it on her coat sleeve, pulling her gently back.

'Wait a minute,' he said, 'those two want to talk over a case—we had better wait here for awhile.'

She stopped and looked at him in amazement. She knew perfectly well that this was only an excuse—they were all 'medicos', and she was quite aware that any of the 'cases' could be discussed freely before Dr Delaney and herself. So taken by surprise was she that speech was impossible for the moment.

'Sit down,' said the other, and she found herself sitting beside him, with a feeling that there was something strange—electrical—in the air around her.

But nothing happened. Dr Delaney talked on very much as usual—in the ordinary friendly 'chummy' way to which she was accustomed when they were alone together—telling her about his visit to Paris a few months previously, and going into raptures, as he generally did, over Napoleon's tomb.

'I would like to show it to you,' he said, 'you would never forget it.'

They were both Bonaparte worshippers—one of the many bonds between them.

'There's a film coming to one of the Picture Houses next week,' he went on, 'some episode in the life of the little King of Rome I believe—we'll go and see it—shall we?'

'I should love it,' said Mary.

'All right—Friday next,'—this was Monday—'will that suit?'

'Perfectly—it's my night off,' said the girl, 'and now don't you think that those two have finished their very private consultation, and that we might join them?'

Dr Delaney hesitated and seemed inclined to say something, but rose to his feet the next minute and followed her from the room, switching off the light as he did so.

Mary turned the handle of the surgery door, and was literally dumbfounded to find it locked. At the same moment a smothered laugh from within fell upon her ears.

She turned in amazement and looked up at Dr Delaney standing tall and silent beside her. She could just see him in the dim light coming in from the street lamp.

'The door,' she gasped, 'it—it's locked.'

'Never mind,' he said, drawing her away—'it's evident that they don't want us yet. We will wait for a few minutes longer—come back to the waiting-room.'

Mary suffered herself to be led back in a sort of dumb surprise. Why on earth was the surgery door locked?

The reason was made clear to her later on by a laughing Nurse Seeley, but at the moment it did not dawn upon her.

Dr Delaney followed her into the room, but did not switch on the light.

Mary waited for a breathless moment, expecting to hear the little click of the switch, and to see the room flooded again with light. But it did not come—instead there was silence—a silence that at last she felt compelled to break.

'Oh, put on the light, *please*,' she said—her voice coming with difficulty in little gasps. (Oh! if she could only see him—what was going to happen?)

'I don't think I'll put the light on again,' was the quiet reply, 'it might bring in more patients if they saw the waiting-room still lit up.'

Then in a softer—dangerously soft voice—'Are you afraid of me in the dark?'

Mary laughed tremulously.

'Not a bit!' she said, trying to speak in her ordinary tones.

'Well, come nearer to me—won't you?'

She endeavoured to laugh again but failed ignominiously. 'I—I can't see you in the dark!' she whispered.

'Well I must help you then,' was the answer, and the next moment she was in his arms.

CHAPTER VIII

CHRISTMAS TIDE

Early the next morning Mary Carmichael was kneeling outside one of the confessionals in the church where the nurses of St Columba's attended for daily Mass. Mary had her regular confessor to whom she had gone for the last two years, but he was not attached to this church. She was particularly sorry that she could not go to him this morning, but had she done so she would have been late for breakfast at the Home, and so it was not to be thought of. She felt a little nervous—in spite of her almost unrealisable happiness—as she knelt there waiting for the priest.

It was a few minutes after seven o'clock, and Mass was being celebrated at the High Altar, and also at two of the side altars. The church was fairly full, and there was a constant stream of worshippers coming and going, and Mary watched them idly. She was trying to concentrate her mind on her prayers, trying to prepare for her Confession, but found it almost impossible to do so. She had hardly closed her eyes during the night but had found herself going over and over again the happy hour in St Paul's Surgery—feeling once more *his* arms around her, *his* kisses on her lips. It had really come to her at last!—this great, this unbelievable happiness at which she had only allowed herself to glance now and then. Sleep kept far off all night, and she only fell into an uneasy doze as it drew towards morning; then soon after six o'clock she rose and dressed herself and took her way to the church for Confession. She had been to the Sacrament of Penance as usual on the previous Saturday and this was only Tuesday, but to Mary, the fact that she had allowed a man to hold her in his arms and to kiss her—even though that man was her future husband—made it necessary for her to get Absolution before she could receive Holy Communion. And she would not have missed receiving on *this* morning for a great deal—this, the Feast of the Immaculate Conception, the end—and oh, what a fitting end, to her Novena.

'Oh, Mother Immaculate,' she whispered, with shining eyes and trembling lips, 'I thank thee, oh, I thank thee.'

The priest was coming, with noiseless sandalled feet, and a soft swish of his flowing habit, and the next minute Mary was at his feet.

'And this man, my daughter—has he a real respect for you—real regard? You are sure his intentions are those of an honourable man?'

'Oh, Father,' and she smiled to herself as she knelt there in the dark interior, 'if you only knew him. He is good—so really good—and the soul of honour and truth—oh, it is I—I'—and her voice faltered, 'Oh, Father it is *I* that am not worthy of him—oh! not worthy at all.'

Another few minutes, and with the last words of the priest's blessing still ringing in her ears Mary was kneeling before Our Lady's Altar, pouring out her soul in gratitude. Afterwards, during her thanksgiving, she felt the tears rush to her eyes for joy—joy that seemed too great to be borne.

'Now I understand why joy sometimes kills,' she said to herself, as she fought hard for composure ere she left the church and returned to St Columba's. There all was as usual—the breakfast-table was just the same. The nurses were just the same and the Matron poured the same watery lotion into their cups under the delusion that she was giving them tea. But to Mary everything seemed different—and she felt more than ever inclined to pinch herself and see if she were really awake or not. She did not know or care what she was eating, but just went mechanically through the routine of the table—even the 'lotion' which she detested from her very heart—passed unnoticed by her this morning. She sat through the short breakfast, almost in silence, with shining eyes, and it was with the utmost difficulty that she forced herself to answer the few remarks addressed to her.

'This is awful,' she thought, with a shamefaced, tender little smile at her own weakness, 'How will I ever get through my work if I let my thoughts wander like this?'

But no sooner was she on duty than she found that the daily routine, the accustomed discipline and above all her love for her work—enabled her to get through her morning's cases without too much day-dreaming.

The next evening she asked leave after supper, which was at the early hour of 8 p.m. at St Columba's, and took the tram across to Rathmines to the Blakes' house. Mary Blake had only to look at her to know what had happened.

'Come up to my room and take off your cloak,' she said, and as they were mounting the stairs she slipped her arm around the other's waist, 'Mary,' she whispered softly, 'it's all right, isn't it? He has spoken to you?'

And Mary Carmichael, 'betwixt smiles and tears,' told her all.

'But don't say anything to anyone else yet,' she added, 'for nothing is made public—it is just between Theo and myself—and you are the only one to whom I have said anything so far.'

'Oh, Mary,' said her friend, 'isn't our Lady good to you! Dr Delaney! Why you should be a proud woman this night!'

'And do you think I'm not!' cried the other, 'but oh, Mary, I am half afraid—for I know—oh, I *know*—that I am not worthy of him—not fit to be his wife.'

But the other gave her a playful little shake.

'Now don't be silly, Mary,' she said, and if the shake was in joke, the tone of voice was serious, 'don't be silly! A good woman is worthy of a good man any day—indeed more than worthy—and Theodore Delaney knows well that you are fit to be the wife of the best man living.'

'Oh! Mary, don't,' cried her friend, and she shivered as with cold, 'don't talk that way! You don't know me!—I'm not really good at all—not *naturally* good, I mean—and it is a hard struggle for me sometimes to lead the life of a good Catholic. And I am afraid—oh, Mary, sometimes *horribly* afraid—that if some great trouble or sorrow was to come upon me I should not be able to bear it in the right spirit!'

Mary Blake looked at her friend with puzzled, troubled eyes for a moment—this was a mood she could not fathom.

'Mary, dear,' she said then, 'don't be foolish! Why should you—now especially when a great joy has come into your life—why should you be thinking of evil fortune? But even if God did send you sorrow—and sure we must all go through our share of it in this life. He would surely send you strength to bear it also.'

Mary Carmichael put her arms around her friend, and laid her head on her shoulder.

'Oh, Mary,' she said, brokenly, 'I hope He will—I hope He will.'

The other kissed her in some bewilderment.

'Mary dearest,' she said, 'you are upset and not yourself. And no wonder after the great event of last Monday! Come downstairs now, or the others will be thinking how selfish I am to keep you so long to myself! And don't be thinking of trouble or misfortune at all. Just look at the bright side of things—and Mary, dear, if ever a woman had cause to be happy, you are that woman tonight.'

And so they went downstairs to join in the gay talk and chatter in the homely dining-room—not so very gay tonight, however, for Nora—happy, irresponsible Nora—was at a dance, and Shamus was absent too.

'He's at a Sinn Féin meeting,' said Mary Blake, pausing for a moment before entering the room, 'and do you know, Mary, I wish he wasn't such an extremist, and so mixed up with these political matters.'

'Oh! nonsense!' said the other Mary, smiling, 'What harm will it do him? Besides he is so obsessed by the Irish question that it would be utterly useless to try and change him.'

'It isn't exactly that we want to change him,' said his sister with a loving smile. 'Dear old Shamus! We wouldn't have him otherwise than what he is for the world—but—but I am afraid sometimes that he will get into trouble with the authorities—do something desperate?'

It was Mary Carmichael's turn to look astonished now.

'Into trouble with the authorities?' she repeated. 'Why, Mary dear, you must be daft to think such a thing. Why, what could he do? Surely,' with a light laugh, 'you don't suppose that we are going to have another '98, do you?'

Mary Blake tried to smile, but failed miserably. Did her deep love for this gallant young brother of her's pierce the veil of the future, and did she see for one brief second, a boyish face pale in death—the cold stare of the wide open eyes—the fair hair matted with blood!

Clare Castlemaine looked up from her embroidery as they entered and gave a little cry of pleasure on seeing Mary Carmichael. They had become great friends, and indeed in some ways Clare found that she could speak more openly to Mary than she could to any of her cousins—Angel always excepted.

'Why, Mary,' she cried now, 'how nice you look. What have you been doing to yourself?'

The other occupants of the room—Mr Blake, Tom, and Angel—all looked up as she spoke, and Mr Blake rising and coming forward with outstretched hands, said, as he pushed Mary gently towards Angel's couch:

'Well, now, I think Mary *always* contrives to look nice.'

Mary thanked him with a smile and a blush as she stooped to kiss

Angel, and Tom Blake, watching her face, felt as though a knife had been suddenly thrust through his heart.

'Delaney has spoken to her,' he thought, and it was a rather pale and stern-faced Tom who took her hand in his the next moment—but his hand clasp was as warm and friendly as ever.

Ah Tom, Tom. There are few like you in this selfish world of ours!

Mary Carmichael could not stay long—just a half hour of chatter and laughter, and then it was time for her to retrace her steps towards St Columba's.

Late that same night Mary Blake stood talking for a few moments in her cousin's bedroom.

'How pretty and happy—almost *too* happy—Mary Carmichael looked tonight,' said Clare, 'one would think she had come in for a big fortune, or some wonderful piece of luck!'

Mary Blake smiled. 'Perhaps she has,' she said, but she did not feel at liberty to say anything more. Clare Castlemaine sighed.

'Some people are born lucky,' she said 'and perhaps she is one of them. But do you know, Mary, that although she is so good and religious and all that, still I always have a queer notion that there is another side altogether to her character, and I believe that if she ever got some big trouble or sorrow—well! I don't believe somehow that her religion would help her at all—indeed I think she would—well, I won't say go to the bad—but I mean something very like it!'

'Clare,' gasped Mary in horror.

'Well, Mary, I can't help thinking so. I may be wrong, but one thing I do know, and that is that if ever Mary Carmichael had a big trouble and came out of it all right—I mean remained as good a Catholic after it as she is now, and so on—Well, it would do more towards my conversion to the Catholic faith than all the preaching of hundred of priests could ever do!

Mary Blake stood for a moment, too surprised to speak, and then she said good-night rather soberly, and left the room, for she was remembering the words of Mary Carmichael, earlier in the evening, 'Oh! Mary, I am afraid—sometimes horribly afraid—that if some great trouble or sorrow were to come upon me I would not be able to bear it in the right spirit!' She went rather slowly down to the dining-room, where she found Tom alone, staring with unseeing eyes at some building plans spread on the table before him. He looked up as his sister entered, and the pain in his honest grey eyes smote her to her heart.

She came to him and slipped her hand through his arm, and laid her sleek, brown head on his shoulder.

'Dear old boy,' she said softly, for there were no secrets between these two.

'Mary,' he said quietly, 'tell me!—has Delaney spoken to her?'

And Mary, recognising his right to put the question, answered, just as quietly, 'Yes, Tom.'

'And she? Ah! I needn't ask,' he said bitterly.

Mary said nothing, but her touch was a caress.

There was silence for a short time between them, and then Tom stooped and kissed the gentle face so near his own.

'Never mind, sister mine!' he said, 'don't worry over me—I'm able to bear it! And I could bear it gladly,' he added, 'if I was only sure that this thing was for her happiness.'

'But, Tom,' said his sister, 'surely you can trust Dr Delaney to make her happy?'

Tom Blake did not reply for a moment, but stood gazing into the fire. Then rousing himself, he gave his shoulders a slight shrug.

'Well!—perhaps so!' he said curtly, and returned to his drawings.

The following weeks passed more or less like a dream to Mary Carmichael. She and Dr Delaney met constantly, and went everywhere together—dances, theatres, and pictures, and also to those various scientific and social lectures, in which both were interested. The nurses at St Columba's chaffed Mary a good deal, but she took none of them into her confidence, except Nurse Seeley and Nurse Ray. Nurse Seeley, of course, had partly guessed how matters were for some time past, and Dr Head—most talkative of men!—had told her much more. As for Daisy Ray, her own love affair made her a sympathetic friend, and she and Mary had many a talk together.

'What are you giving Dr Delaney for his Christmas gift, Mac?' inquired Miss Ray one evening, as the two of them were returning homewards along O'Connell Street.

It was within ten days of the great festival now, and the shop windows were glittering with their usual display of Yuletide articles.

'That's just what I am trying to determine, Daisy,' said Mary, with a little sigh of perplexity; 'it is so hard to think of a present for a man! Now for a woman's gift one has almost a limitless choice, but for men!—What are you giving to Brendan?'

'A dressing case,' answered Daisy Ray. 'Yes—I know its extravagant,' as Mary gave a slight exclamation of surprise—'Horribly so for a poor nurse—but you see, dear, it's the first present I am giving him since our engagement, and so I want it to be rather extra special, you know!' and she laughed happily.

Mary laughed too—but also sighed a little to herself. Nurse Ray's engagement was now public property, and off duty she proudly displayed a pretty little engagement ring; but Dr Delaney had not said a word to Mary about announcing theirs. True, it was only a few weeks since he had spoken to her, and of course there was no hurry, still——

But, no doubt, he knew best, and she was content to leave the matter in his hands, where indeed she was content now to leave the whole ordering of her life.

But Daisy was chatting away at her side, like the little magpie she was.

'I'll tell you two things not to give him anyway, Mac,' she was saying. 'Don't give him any kind of a knife or scarf pin, and—oh! yes—don't give him a *prayer book*! You are both such pious creatures you know, that you might be fancying a present of that sort!'

Mary smiled. 'Well, I *was* thinking of a scarf pin,' she admitted.

'Oh, *don't*, Mac!' cried her friend, in tones of exaggerated horror, 'it's most awfully unlucky to give such a thing to anyone you are really fond of.'

'Well, what about sleeve-links?' asked Mary, 'I saw some very pretty ones the other day—gold shamrocks—rather dainty I thought.'

'The very thing!' exclaimed her friend, '*links* you know, bind things together, and the shamrock is for luck—Oh! they will be just right, Mary.'

And so Mary purchased her sleeve-links with a shy joy, and hid them away in her 'bottom drawer' until a few days before Christmas. Then one evening when she and Dr Delaney were going to the pictures together, she took them out, and slipped them into an envelope. Inside she wrote—'Just to wish you a very happy Christmas and a lucky New Year.—Mary.'

And sealing it up she put it in her coat pocket. She and Dr Delaney walked home together from the pictures, and as usual stopped for a last few moments' conversation under the street lamp in the old Square. Across the wide street was St Columba's Home, the light from the lamp flickering on its wide front, and great stone steps, flickering too on the shining, wet pavement under their feet, for it had been raining. How often they had stood there of a night! 'Their lamp,' they called it. The policeman, whose beat was on that side of the Square, knew them well, and often threw them a sympathetic smile, as he saluted in passing.

Mary felt a little shy and nervous as her hand sought her coat pocket.

'I have a little thing for you—for Christmas,' she said, with a shakey laugh—'something I got in the Penny Bazaar for you. You are not to open it till you get home!'

His fingers closed on hers as he took the little gift and seemed reluctant to let them go. Then he also dived into a pocket and brought forth a package.

'I didn't know what in the world to get you,' he said, 'and then I got this, and put it in my pocket tonight to give you; but someway I thought you mightn't care for it, and I was nearly going to bring it back home with me.'

He was unwrapping the package as he spoke, and drew forth a fountain pen.

'This is the kind I use myself,' he said, 'it is not the usual sort, and I want to explain it to you—indeed the young man in the shop told me to be sure and give the lady a demonstration before she started using it herself. I was rather amused at him taking it for granted that it was intended for a lady friend.'

Then unscrewing the pen, he showed Mary how to fill it, and screw it—how it was to be cleaned and so on.

And Mary listened with a smiling face and with pretty words of thanks—but with just a tiny pang of disappointment. She tried not to feel it—not to think of it—but it came back to her again and again, as she lay sleepless through the small hours.

No! she had *not* expected a fountain pen—she had hoped for something very different. Then she began to worry over the sleeve-links. Would he think it forward of her? Perhaps she shouldn't have given him anything—no jewellery anyway? She tossed and turned and worried, but could not find an answer to her perplexities!

But in the morning, as is usual with us all, she felt fifty times better and brighter, and when later in the day, Theodore Delaney rang her up to thank her for the links, and to tell her how delighted he was with them—although he scolded her a little too—and that he was going to a medical dinner that night, when he would wear them, she felt at peace with herself and the world once more.

And so the great festival of Christmas came round, and Clare Castlemaine in a letter to Mrs Webb, told her first impressions of an Irish Catholic Christmas:

> DEAREST OLD WEBBIE,
>
> Well! Christmas has come and gone once more, and I am writing as I promised, to tell you how I spent it here. It was the strangest, and yet the most beautiful Yuletide I ever spent in my life. You know, Webbie dear, I rather dreaded it because I thought it would be rather sad for me without dear father. Not that Christmas ever meant anything to him—he often described it to me as 'a modern orgy of over-eating and over-drinking, by which the Christians of today celebrate the birth of their Founder,' and he would often add, 'that if their Founder was on earth today He would not own them as His followers.' And then, too, I thought I would miss my own home. But my cousins seemed to guess what was in my mind, and they simply vied with one another trying to make me happy, and above all to make me feel at home. What will you say when I tell you that I started the day by going to High Mass at six o'clock. I did feel so funny getting up so soon after 5 a.m.—it was so dark and cold. But I was the only one who seemed to feel it—none of the others gave a thought to such a material thing as atmospheric conditions! They appeared to be treading on air—so happy were they all. I don't know that I can tell you exactly how the ceremony of the Mass struck me, because I didn't understand it. It was what they call 'High Mass,' and there were three priests celebrating, and a lot more seemed to be about, also the laybrothers of the Order. The music was exquisite, and they sang some carols, I have heard before in England, and also the hymn 'Come all ye Faithful,' but they sang it in Latin of course. What really impressed me was the huge crowd of communicants. I never saw such a sight in my life before, and you would want to see it yourself dearest, to understand the effect it had on me.

Certainly, whether they are right or wrong, Catholics do believe the teaching of their Church. I watched them going up to the Altar and returning to their places, and I never saw such faith and devotion, such love and reverence shown before—their very faces seemed to shine with the thought of what they were doing! It is a mystery to me. Webbie, but there must be something in this religion of theirs, the way it seems to permeate their whole life, and after all my own mother knew all about it and loved it—didn't she? Oh! Webbie, sometimes I wish I had her faith! I could not help feeling so out of it in the Church that morning. But when we got home—such laughter and fun—such giving of gifts! Simple little things, all of them, but showing such loving thought and planning. I was ashamed that I was able to give them better presents than they gave me, for you know I hardly ever have to spend here, and I have plenty of spare cash yet. Things are so different here where a sovereign is regarded as riches untold!

Well! We had a happy Christmas, and in the evening—dinner was at seven o'clock—Mary Carmichael came, and also Mr Anthony Farrell—of whom, I think, I told you before. Dr Delaney had to go to his mother and sisters, who live somewhere in Terenure direction. To tell you the truth, I was rather surprised that he didn't ask Mary Carmichael to spend Christmas with his people, for I imagine that they are now practically engaged, and I think she felt a bit disappointed but she was quite jolly in spite of it—indeed, everyone was in high spirits. Such a gay dinner, Webbie, and yet not half as elaborate as we are accustomed to on the other side of the water and yet twice as happy. That is what impressed me the most of all this Christmas—the importance attached to the spiritual side of the Festival. In England it always seemed to me that the so-called Christians simply regarded Christmas as a time for eating and drinking more than usual—but here, all that comes secondary to the great religious aspect of the Feast. They never seem to forget here that it is a holy sacred time, a time for rejoicing and gaiety certainly—but all within limits.

Now Webbie, I am tired, so good-bye for the present, and write soon again to

Yours lovingly,

CLARE.

CHAPTER IX

'LENT'

The first few months of 1914 passed uneventfully for all our friends. How little did people imagine what that year was to bring forth, and what terrible devastation and bloodshed would overwhelm Europe before its close.

Clare Castlemaine had quite settled down with her cousins and daily grew fonder of them all, so that the thought of leaving them became very painful to her. Still to continue as their guest for an indefinite period was out of the question. Although not poor, neither were they wealthy, and even though so many of the family were earning, still she knew that the expenses of the household must be fairly heavy. So after a pretty hard tussle both with her uncle and with Mary, Clare gained her point, and it was settled that she should remain as a paying guest for as long as she liked. She was perfectly content from that on, and threw herself more fully into the life around her.

Perhaps of all her cousins—except Angel who always remained her favourite—she liked Shamus the best. There was something so gay and boyish about him, he was so full of fun—so fond of teasing, and yet withal so tender and considerate—that to his half-English cousin he proved an irresistible mixture. He was an ardent Catholic, as she knew, but some of his dearest friends were amongst the non-Catholic sects, and she had never heard a bigoted or intolerant speech from his lips. He took to Clare from the first, and now that she felt equal to going about more, he often asked her to accompany him in the evenings. They went to the Abbey Theatre together, and there Clare for the first time saw Irish plays acted by Irish players, and laughed at the remembrance of the 'stage Irishman' whom she had sometimes seen on the London boards. She went, too, with him to various meetings—Norah Donovan and Anthony Farrell generally accompanying them—and there she heard speeches from men whose names were destined to be written on the pages of Irish history later on, although neither she nor they guessed it then. She began to understand—as she had thought she never could—the Irish point of view, and to look at things in general from an Irish stand-point. But all this was not easy and took time, for when one has been accustomed all one's life to gaze upon the world with the serene and placid stupidity of the average Englishman, it is rather puzzling to suddenly find oneself gazing at the same world from a totally different vantage ground.

Her friendship with Anthony Farrell progressed rapidly, in fact it had gone beyond the bounds of friendship, as each of them knew in their heart. The Blakes knew this also, and rejoiced greatly, Shamus especially, for as he said to Norah, 'If *anyone* can eradicate her unfortunate English blood, and make Clare into a decent Catholic Irishwoman—that one is Anthony Farrell!'

As for Shamus and Norah they had been sweethearts since they were children together, but they knew that they would have to remain sweethearts for some years yet, before they could attain to that ideal little home which the two of them were busy planning in their own minds. But they were young and strong—full of hope and energy, and so content to wait.

Oh! Blessed be God! Who in His infinite mercy ordains that the future is hidden from us!

As for Mary Carmichael she seemed to be living in a happy dream most of her time. St Columba's with its rigid rules, hard work, and monotonous food became for her a veritable Paradise on earth. In the morning she thought, 'I will see him today!' or if they were not to meet—'I will talk to him over the 'phone—I will at least hear his voice!'

And she was full of such a deep gratitude, such a fervent love for God who had been so good to her that she seemed as if she could never do enough for Him now. 'Oh! if I could only show Him how grateful I am! If I could only do something to prove my love for Him!' She used to think many a time.

And then when Lent drew near a sudden thought entered her mind. But it was a thought that she would not harbour at first, for it brought with it pain—pain and self-sacrifice. But the thought returned again and again with a persistency that would not be gainsaid, and at last Mary found herself compelled to give it house-room.

And this idea that filled her mind with such a strange mixture of joy and pain—what was it? Nothing more or less than the resolution to give up all communication or intercourse of any kind whatsoever with Theodore Delaney during the time of Lent—not to meet him or to write to him—not even to 'ring him up' on the overworked 'phone at St Columba's. From Shrove Tuesday until Easter they were to renounce each other, and to become as strangers.

But even as she was making up her mind to this penance, she shrank from the very thought. But over and over again she found herself thinking 'God had been so good to me—so good—so good—can I not do this for Him! Just to give up what I love best for six weeks? What is it after all when I am to have him afterwards for all my life!'

And still she faltered at the thought of the ordeal—for that it would be a bit of real self-sacrifice she knew but too well. Not to see his beloved face—not to hear his dear voice, for six long weeks! Could she do it? For her Divine Lord—yes! Otherwise it would have been impossible to her.

She broached the subject one night to Dr Delaney, as they were taking a long walk together near Ballsbridge.

'What are you going to give up for Lent?' she asked him.

'Well now, that's just what I was considering a few days ago,' he answered, 'I suppose we will have to forego theatres and the pictures—eh?'

Oh! that little word 'we'—how it pierced her heart tonight!

'Oh, of course,' she said, 'but that's nothing! I always give them up—don't you? But I have been thinking, then, that this Lent, as God has been so good to us—Well, I was thinking that we ought to do *something* a little harder.'

Dr Delaney looked down at her whimsically. 'Well, what do you want me to do?' he asked teasingly. 'Live on bread and water, or give up smoking? I'd prefer the former, although as a matter of fact, I always limit my tobacco fairly strictly during Lent.'

'No, I don't want you to live on bread and water, or do without your pipe,' said Mary, 'but—but I thought perhaps that you could do without me.'

Theodore Delaney almost stopped on the footpath to stare at her.

'Do without you, Mary?' he asked, 'what on earth do you mean?'

Then she explained to him, and told him what she was planning for Lent. As she had expected, it did not meet with his approval, and he argued against it pretty strongly, but in the end he found himself unable to hold out against Mary's unanswerable plea—'Our dear Lord has done so much for us!—can't we do this one little thing for Him?'

And so it was arranged. From Shrove Tuesday night until Easter Saturday morning, they were to be absolutely separated. But on Easter Saturday morning at 9 a.m., he was to ring her up on the telephone, and in the evening they would meet once more!

'That's if we are both alive, you wicked girl!' said Dr Delaney, 'six weeks, why it will be an eternity!'

Mary laughed too, but rather shakily.

'You may send me something for the fifteenth,' she said.

The fifteenth of March was the day on which Mary Carmichael had been received into the Catholic Church, and to her it was always a very special day of thanksgiving and rejoicing. Also on that day she was accustomed to get little gifts and congratulatory notes from those of her friends who were really intimate with her.

'Well! I wasn't likely to forget that day, Mary,' said Theodore, 'and I suppose I may write—just a little note?'

'No, don't write,' she said, 'but you may send me a new prayer book—I want one very badly. Get me a copy of 'the Flowers of Nazareth'—I never use any other. But you know, dear, I won't acknowledge it—only it will make me so happy to know that you remembered me on that day.'

They were to meet for the last time before their voluntary separation, on Shrove Tuesday, and as on that day both happened to be very busy—Dr Delaney especially so—it was late in the afternoon when he rang up Mary on the telephone.

'I have to go to Terenure this evening, can't get out of it,' he told her over the wire. 'Could you be at Harcourt Street station at ten o'clock? I know it's rather late, but I can't possibly manage to meet you any earlier.'

Of course she would be there! Where and at what hour would she not have gone to meet him on this—their last—night?

It was just ten o'clock when Mary left the tram at Harcourt Street railway station. It had been raining all evening—a cold drizzle, unpleasant and depressing. She took her stand under the clock from which she could see the various trams passing and re-passing on the street, and at seven minutes past ten she espied Dr Delaney's well-known figure and familiar walk, as he crossed the street towards her from a Terenure car.

They shook hands almost in silence—the gloom of the night seemed to have affected them both.

'Rotten evening—isn't it?' he said, and Mary assenting in silence, they started to walk down Harcourt Street together.

Neither of them mentioned a tram, or thought of such a thing—both had taken trams on their way to meet each other, but they started to walk to St Columba's as a matter of course. Surely their time together was short enough tonight without taking a tram!

Altogether it was rather a silent walk. They spoke but little, and that on impersonal matters, until they came within sight of St Columba's.

Then complete silence fell upon them, and they walked twice round the square without exchanging a word. But time was passing—it was close on eleven o'clock, and Mary knew that she dare not be any later entering the Home.

So they stopped by tacit consent at the usual lamp-post and the woman spoke first, wistfully, sadly, all the love of her heart looking out of her grey eyes, as she glanced up at the man beside her.

'Will you miss me during the coming weeks?' she asked, the words almost a whisper.

'You know I will,' he answered, and then added abruptly. 'Mary, is your mind really made up on this matter? Are you resolved that we are not to meet at all till Easter?'

'Yes, Theo. You know I am.'

'Well! look here—you are running a risk, you know!'

'Running a risk?' And Mary repeated the words in a sort of stupid wonder. 'Running a risk? What on earth do you mean?'

Dr Delaney laughed uneasily.

'Oh, well, you see,' he said, 'I mightn't want to be friends again after Lent! Six weeks is a long time you know!'

Mary stared at him for a moment, and then she laughed.

It was Theo's teasing way of course!—he was such a great tease.

He laughed also, but added, half jokingly, half seriously, 'But suppose that this absence was to cause a change of feeling with me—would you still adhere to this resolution of yours?'

For just a moment Mary hesitated. Then she lifted her head a little proudly, 'I would!' she answered, 'for a friendship that could not remain unchanged through a six-week's separation would not be worth keeping.'

Dr Delaney laughed again, but not very naturally.

'Well, remember that I've warned you—that's all!' he said.

And Mary, taking it all as a huge joke, laughed back, and said that she would certainly remember.

A few minutes more and they had separated. Just a lingering hand-clasp, a long look into each other's eyes, and then Mary was stumbling up the stone steps and feeling for her latch-key with trembling fingers. She thrust it into the key-hole and entered the Home, without trusting herself to give one backward glance towards the tall figure in the street below.

Oh, but the hundred stairs up to her bedroom seemed very long and weary that night, and when she reached her room at last she was thankful to find that Nurse Jackson was in bed and sound asleep. Mary undressed with shaking fingers, and kneeling down before her little picture of the Sacred Heart she tried to pray. But she was over-wrought, and had to give up the attempt—still she knelt on for some time looking up at the Divine Face through a mist of tears.

'Oh, Sacred Heart!' she breathed again and again. 'Help me to bear it! Help me to bear it! Not to see him!—not to speak to him—to know nothing of him except by hearsay—for six weeks, six *weeks*! Oh, how will I do it! How *can* I bear it!' And then again, more tenderly, more lovingly, 'Dear Lord, it is for Thee!—it is for Thee!' And so at last, sadly and wearily she crept to bed. Of course the next morning her first waking thought was—'I won't see him today!' and her next, 'nor tomorrow, nor the next day, and oh, nor for weeks and weeks.' The she made the Sign of the Cross and an Act of Contrition, and during Mass she prayed really earnestly that she might not think too much of him during that day, and all the following days of Lent, but bear patiently her self-chosen cross.

It was a gloomy, dismal day, and the faces of the nurses gathered round the breakfast table that morning seemed to be in unison with the weather. Dry toast and black tea, no matter how spiritual we may be, are not conducive to gaiety or good spirits. Mary Carmichael detested 'black' fast days; indeed, she had found it rather hard to fast or abstain at any time, not having been brought up to it. Not that she was a large eater or cared much for elaborate meals, but as she used to say laughingly, 'I like a little and often!'

Of course she couldn't bear the food at St Columba's, and had her own special tea shop in her district where she could get a dainty little tea if time permitted her to break her morning fast. But alas, she remembered that there could be no such indulgence in these luxuries today—she could take nothing until she came back to the dry fish dinner at two o'clock.

It was when she was returning from her evening visits about six o'clock that she saw him—and strange to say she never saw him again during Lent. And yet it was hardly so strange either, for both of them knew each other's haunts and would be pretty certain to keep away from those places where they would be likely to encounter one another—for so much 'was in the bond'.

But on Ash Wednesday night Mary saw him quite unexpectedly. She was seated in a tram gazing idly out on the wet pavements, shining under the street lamps. The street was, of course, very crowded at that hour, principally with people homeward bound to the various suburbs and trying to board trams and get cover from the heavy rain. Mary's tram was coming down Dame Street, and at the corner of South George's Street, Dr Delaney was standing. Her heart gave a sudden sickening throb as she saw him, and the tram stopping for a moment to take up a passenger, she was able to observe him fairly closely, and she noticed how sad and utterly weary he looked, staring straight in front of him, but as one whose thoughts were far away. If Mary Carmichael lived to be a hundred years old, she would never forget the pain at her heart, and the unutterable, overwhelming desire she experienced to leave the car and cross over to him, to slip her hand through his arm in the dear old way, and to say to him—'Theo, I'm here; I can't go on with this thing—I can't do without you even for six weeks. Let us give it up!'

She almost rose from her seat and had to exert all her will power not to get out. The next moment the car was moving on, and the temptation had passed, but it had left her so physically sick and weak that she feared she would faint. She saw a gentleman on the opposite seat looking keenly at her—she knew him by sight as a medical man—and with a tremendous effort she pulled herself together and managed to shake off the deadly faintness that had been stealing over her.

She was wretched in mind and body when she reached St Columba's.

'Oh, God forgive me,' she thought drearily, 'but I don't feel spiritually minded at all—just the very opposite. I'm cold and hungry and miserably unhappy—and I'd like all kinds of things which I can't get, and oh! I want *him!* I want *him!*'

The Lent that followed was long and dreary to Mary, but no day in it was so black or so long to her as this Ash Wednesday. After a comparatively short time she became more reconciled—or rather more accustomed—to that terrible blank in her life which only one person could fill, and soon came the cheerful thought that every day that passed was slowly but surely making her time of penance shorter. Each night as she went to bed she would stroke off the date on her calendar and count the remaining days, till Easter, and after a couple of weeks as they began to get less and less, so in proportion did Mary's spirits rise higher and higher. For the self-sacrifice had been very great, and after all the woman was only human. Still she did try to keep Lent well. Every morning saw her receiving Holy Communion, and sometime during the day, no matter how busy she might be, she would manage to find time for the Stations of the Cross. She prayed earnestly before the Blessed Sacrament, she meditated, she denied herself in many little ways—such as giving up all sweets and cakes, and similar small luxuries.

And so the fifteenth of March arrived and Mary Carmichael remembered with a little thrill of joy that on that day she would receive the prayer-book which Dr Delaney had promised to send her.

She found it on the hall table when she returned from Mass on that morning. It was wrapped in soft tissue paper and carefully packed in a square card-board box—and her heart leapt within her as she recognised the dear familiar hand-writing.

All through breakfast it lay beside her place and her eyes were drawn to it again and again, much to the secret amusement of Daisy Ray. Immediately after breakfast Mary fled with her treasure upstairs. Reverently she untied the string and took off the paper covering reverently and lovingly, for had not his dear hands touched it—handled it? When at last the wrappings were all off and the book lay disclosed to her view she could hardly see it for the rush of tears that came unbidden to her eyes, but she laid it gently against her soft cheek, as she murmured again and again, 'Dear little book, dear little book. I wonder does your sender know how much I really love him?'

That was Mary's 'half-day' and she started off about five o'clock in the afternoon to pay a visit to a convent in the suburbs, where lived the Sister of Charity who had instructed her in the doctrine of the Church and had prepared her for her Reception into the true fold. This nun had always remained one of Mary's best and truest friends—in the real sense of the word—and Mary tried to see her pretty frequently. However, it was now some months since she had seen her last, but on this day she would not have missed a talk with Sister Joseph for a good deal. It was a lovely day, with a real feeling of spring in the atmosphere to which Mary was quick to respond. The birds were singing in the trees of the long avenue which led up to the convent, and her heart was singing with them.

The Sister was seated in her special little sanctum, where she saw 'her girls' in the evenings.

'Ah, Mary,' she said, as her visitor entered, 'I was expecting you this evening—and just thinking of you.'

'Did you remember what day it was, Sister?' Mary asked happily.

'Of course, I did, my child. Do I ever forget it? But how well and happy you look. God bless you, dearie, and send you many happy anniversaries of this day,' and the Sister took the smiling face between her hands and kissed her, nun fashion, on both cheeks.

'And now sit down, and tell me all your news,' she said, and the next moment Mary was chatting away with real pleasure, for she had a very deep affection for Sister Joseph.

'By the way, what about your Novena for the Feast of the Immaculate Conception?' asked the nun. 'I meant to have asked you about it several times, but always forgot. You promised to tell me if you obtained what you were praying for—although you would not let me know what those intentions were.'

Mary's face crimsoned in spite of all her efforts to keep cool, as she said, 'Oh, Sister, I got my intention. Such a wonderful answer came to my prayers. Some day you will know all, but it is a secret just yet—a secret between myself and one other.'

The Sister smiled, and glanced at Mary quizzically over her glasses.

'Suppose I know who the other person is?' she queried, and then as Mary sat in dumb surprise, she added quietly, 'Dr Delaney was with me this morning.'

Mary caught her breath sharply, and it was a minute or two before she could speak, then she asked shyly, 'Did he tell you, Sister?'

Sister Joseph nodded her head briskly.

'Not that I needed much telling, dear,' she said. 'Do you suppose I have been blind for the last two years?—knowing you both as well as I do I could hardly fail to see how things were going. My only wonder is that everything wasn't settled long ago.'

'Oh, Sister,' breathed Mary, 'did you really guess? Why I didn't know myself until he spoke to me—in fact I didn't dare think of such a thing.'

'My dear child—why not?'

'Oh, just because I—I thought it would be too good to be true, the happiness would be too great. I could not believe that such a thing would ever come to pass in this sorry old world.' But the nun only smiled as she said, 'Well, you see, dear child, that it has come to pass. And I am so glad, Mary. I cannot tell you, dear, how thankful I am that God has been so good to you. But you deserve it all!—yes, every bit,' as Mary lifted a protesting hand, '—every bit, dearie—for you are a good woman and, please God, you will make a good and loving wife.'

Mary's eyes were misty, as she stretched out her hand and laid it for a moment on Sister Joseph's.

'He always said *you* would be the very first to know it,' she whispered.

Then the ice being broken, she opened her heart to this old friend of hers, and told her some of her hopes and fears for the future, of her gratitude to God, and of her Lenten Penance.

'But Lent is passing quickly now, Sister!' she added, in tones of such heartfelt relief that the nun had hard work to keep from laughing—for Sister Joseph understood poor human nature and was never severe on its limitations. Mary rose to go shortly afterwards, and the Sister went with her to the door. She paused for a moment on the threshold and put her hands on Mary's shoulder.

'Mary,' she said, 'don't make an idol of Theodore Delaney. From a mere worldly point of view it is unwise for a woman to make too much of any man—no matter how near perfection she may consider him. And then, well, dear, even he—precious as he is to you—must not come before your Divine Lord.'

And then before Mary could reply she kissed her softly and closed the door.

Mary walked down the convent avenue as though she trod on air—a little bird was singing in her heart and his song was louder than that of any of the feathered songsters, thrilling out their evening hymns all around her.

So he had spoken to Sister and told her the great news, yes, he had always said that Sister Joseph should be the first to know. As for the nun's warning to her not to make an idol of this man she loved—Mary only smiled to herself. He *was* her idol, and she knew it. But she could not help worshipping him as she did, and besides—there were no clay feet to her idol.

On the top of the tram she encountered Tom Blake.

His face lit up at the sight of her.

'Why Mary, where have you sprang from?' he inquired, as they shook hands.

'Oh, Tom,' she cried happily, 'is it you? I was only up at the convent seeing Sister Joseph. Isn't it a glorious evening? Spring has come already.'

'Yes, it's a ripping evening,' Tom assented quietly, 'and how are you, Mary? I haven't seen you this good while.'

'No—you were out the last time I was in Rathmines,' said Mary, 'and then I haven't been going out much—Lent you know. But I'm quite well, and as fit as a fiddle, thank you,' smiling at him with dancing eyes.

'You look it,' said Tom, 'although I think you've got a trifle thinner than you were. Don't over-do it, Mary, and kill yourself altogether.'

Mary laughed gaily. 'No fear,' she said, 'life is too wonderful for one to want to leave it yet awhile.' Tom smiled, rather sadly.

'How transparent she is,' he thought, 'one could imagine she was a girl in her teens, she seems so young and joyous these days.'

'I suppose you are not indulging in much gaiety either, Tom?' she asked presently. 'Will you be at the Nurses' Dance on St Patrick's night?'

'No,' he said, 'I don't dance in Lent—but I hear it's to be a very big affair?'

'Yes, we have sold nearly four hundred tickets. Of course most of the nurses in the Home are going—all of them in fact, except Daisy Ray and yours truly. We are going to be the sensible ones and stay at home. Well, Tom—I must get down here. Good-bye and give my love to all at home,' and with a gay wave of the hand, Mary ran down the steps and got off the car. She turned to wave to him again from the road, and then she disappeared round a corner, and for Tom the spring atmosphere went with her, and only a cold, grey March evening was left behind.

CHAPTER X

'CAN THIS THING BE?'

Although Mary Carmichael had spoken lightly enough to Tom Blake about foregoing the Nurses' Dance on the 17th, it was still a great piece of self-sacrifice. She would not have minded it so much if she had not been living in the Home, where the dance just then was almost the sole topic of conversation.

Mary was so popular, too, that each nurse insisted on showing her the evening gown, slippers, gloves, etc., that were intended for the great night, and Mary with that true sympathy which was one of her most attractive qualities, admired and criticised, and helped with all these details.

On the afternoon of the 17th, she strolled into the Recreation Room at St Columba's to see them all having their 'hair done'. Two hairdressers were there and all the nurses were seated round with their scanty or luxurious locks—as the case might be—hanging around their shoulders, awaiting their turn, while the two 'under treatment' at the moment were submitting to the ordeal of having their hair curled and waved and crimped, and arranged according to the latest fashionable decree.

'Do look at Nurse Breen!' said Mary softly to Nurse Ray, who, like herself, was merely a spectator. 'She looks quite frightened! What on earth does she think the poor man is going to do to her?'

Daisy laughed. 'Oh! well, she's a regular country girl you know,' she said, 'and she wasn't even trained in town—some small country infirmary. I suppose she never had her hair dressed before and is a bit dubious over it.'

'I suppose so,' assented Mary, adding after a moment, 'do you ever think Daisy, how awful it would be to live in the country?'

'Well it wouldn't suit *you* , Mac—that's sure!' said the other.

'I should think not!' said Mary, 'I was in the country once—for a month—in the summer too, when I suppose I should have enjoyed it, and I *never* was so utterly bored and wretched in my whole life! I can't tell you how my heart leapt for joy simply to hear the jangle of the dear old trams again, and the shouts of the newsboys, the evening I arrived back at Kingsbridge.'

'Oh, yes,' replied Daisy, 'as I said Mac, it wouldn't suit you at all—you are essentially a city sparrow, but plenty of people like country life.'

'Life?' repeated Mary, scornfully. 'It wouldn't be *living*—it would be simply stagnation—why, I should just feel as if I were turned into a cabbage for the rest of my days!'

'Oh, well, Mac,' she said, 'it's not likely that you will ever have to spend your days in the country. I think Dr Delaney hates it too?'

'Oh, yes,' said Mary, 'he detests it! Neither of us are happy off the tram line!' and with a gay laugh she left the room to get ready for her evening work, as she had promised to visit some of the more urgent cases of those nurses who were going to the dance.

She was back in fairly good time, and stood in the hall watching the bustle of departure—taxi after taxi driving up and going off with its burden of radiant nurses. Involuntarily Mary sighed. She thought of the Aberdeen Hall with its perfect floor, the lights and music—she could imagine herself whirling round in the gay throng, the gayest of the gay, for Mary always danced—as she did everything else—with all her heart. And then the supper, and the sitting out with him. 'Oh! well he won't be there anyhow! I'm sure of that!' she said to herself, and turned to meet Daisy Ray's rather quizzical glance.

'Regretting you resolution, Mac?'

But Mary shook her head.

'No,' she said, 'I'm not—not really. But, of course, I cannot help wishing in a way that I was going off for a night's enjoyment. And you know, Daisy, how I just love a dance!'

'Oh, yes, I know,' said the other tranquilly, 'I used to feel that way too, but somehow now—since Brendan doesn't dance—I don't seem to care about it. Dr Delaney does dance, I know,' she added, 'but, of course he won't be there tonight?'

'Oh, no, he won't be there,' said Mary, and the two stay-at-homes returned to the deserted sitting room together. The room looked strangely untidy and unlike itself. Scraps of ribbon and lace were thrown here and there, chairs were out of their places, and an odd glove and some flowers—evidently forgotten by one of the nurses—lay on the table, Mary went round putting things straight in a mechanical fashion, while Daisy watched her idly from the hearthrug.

'Mac,' she said, suddenly, 'Brendan is coming in tonight for a while. You don't mind?'

'Mind?' said Mary. 'My goodness—no! why should I?' Of course this was strictly against the rules, no gentlemen visitors being admitted at St Columba's. But tonight when the Matron and nurses were going to the dance, and both the cook and housemaid were off for the evening, Daisy had evidently considered that she might do worse than allow her fiancé within the sacred precincts of the Home for a short time.

Just then the door bell rang.

'There he is! Let him in, Daisy' said Mary laughingly; but it was not Brendan Kelly who accompanied Nurse Ray back to the sitting room, but a Nurse Maguire who worked under one of the many Insurance Societies in the city.

Mary Carmichael had not met her before, and came forward now with her winning smile, as Daisy made the necessary introduction—which she did in her own way.

'This is Nurse Maguire, Mac,' she said, 'she thought she would be in time to see the others going off to the dance—and Maguire, this is Nurse Carmichael—*the* Carmichael you know; you've often heard of her!' she added with a laugh. Nurse Maguire smiled as she shook hands with Mary.

'Oh, yes, indeed! I have very often heard of Nurse Carmichael,' she said; 'a certain medical man of my acquaintance often speaks of her.'

Mary coloured vividly and was about to reply when the bell rang again, and Daisy went to the door, returning in a minute with Brendan Kelly. He shook hands with the other two in his pleasant, boyish way, and then they all grouped round the fire, laughing and chatting.

But presently Mary—whose fellow feeling made her wondrously kind—proposed that she and Nurse Maguire should descend to the kitchen regions and there see what they could discover in the way of an impromptu supper. So, with the visitor, she descended the dark, stone steps leading into the cook's department, and there after a diligent forage Mary came upon some sausages and tomatoes and some cold potatoes.

'What luck!' she cried, 'I wonder how cook came to leave them out of the safe—which, of course, is locked as usual! Anne is right about Martha—she is an old miser!'

She bustled around, and very soon an appetising if homely little meal was prepared.

'I'll take up a tray to the two in the sitting-room,' she said to Nurse Maguire, 'and let them have it to themselves, and we will have ours down here—if you don't mind?'

'Of course I don't,' replied the other nurse, who while watching Mary's happy face and quick, deft movements, had found herself becoming fascinated by that indefinite charm which Mary exercised over so many.

So a supper tray was gaily loaded with sausages, mashed potatoes and tomatoes—and of course the inevitable teapot—and Mary went upstairs with it.

When she returned she gaily dispensed the same luxuries to Nurse Maguire and herself, and they sat and talked round the homely kitchen table as if they had been friends for years.

Presently the door bell rang again, and Mary stopped to listen with her tea cup poised in her hand—the nurses at St Columba's always felt guilty when drinking tea in the kitchen. Daisy Ray's light feet could be heard running across the hall, then as the door opened she gave a slight exclamation, and the next moment the sound of rather unsteady, shuffling footsteps were distinguished making their way towards the kitchen stairs.

'Oh!' said Mary Carmichael, 'it's Anne! *and she's been at it again.*'

Nurse Maguire glanced at her interrogatively, and Mary nodded.

'Yes,' she said curtly, 'Jameson's J.J.—and after all she promised!'

The unsteady footsteps were coming nearer, and presently the figure of Anne could be discerned lurching in a sailor-like fashion round the corner by the last step, and coming slowly but surely towards the kitchen. She wore a tight black skirt and a smart coat, while her Sunday 'toque' composed of black velvet, scarlet geraniums and blue ribbon—and of which she was intensely proud—was tilted at a precarious angle to the side of her head. Her hands were encased in black kid gloves, and in one of them she clasped her beaded handbag, and in the other her umbrella.

She advanced towards the kitchen table, smiling benevolently.

'Supper,' she said then, 'and why not? *Why not* I say! God knows it's not often, Nurse darlint, that you can get a bit to eat in peace, and now that the ould divil is out—' she paused and glanced apprehensively around as though suspecting that the cook might be lurking in some dim recess of the great kitchen. Although well under the influence the fact did not betray itself much in her speech except for a certain thickness.

'Anne,' said Mary, reproachfully, 'how could you? And after all you promised me!'

The culprit turned her eyes towards Mary, with a would-be innocent expression, which however was rather spoiled by their decidedly fishy look. 'What is it , my darlint girl?' she demanded, 'What are you saying at all? Is it *you* that's speaking like that to your poor Anne that would lie down and let you walk over her dead body this holy and blessed St Patrick's night.'

'I don't ask you to let me walk over your body at all,' replied Mary severely, 'all I did ask you to do was to keep sober, and you know you promised me that tonight especially you would not——'

'Sober is it?' interrupted the innocent one, 'and what more sober could I be than what I am at this blessed minute? Two cups of tea and a bottle of lemon soda at me sister's, and she after burying the second twin last week, the poor misfortunate woman, and her husband after——'

But at this moment the heavy and ponderous step of Martha the cook was heard descending the stairs.

Martha was a country woman and looked askance at all Dubliners, just as they in their turn looked contemptuously at her. She was a strict teetotaller, and a perfect miser in her own way, putting nearly all her wages in the Post Office. She carried her parsimonious habits into St Columba's too, and cut and pared the contents of the larder in a most niggardly style. She detested Anne and regarded her as an extravagant flighty woman, who spent her money on drink and theatres and picture houses, when, instead, she should be saving for that old age which was not so far off, whilst Anne in her turn hated Martha, as 'an ould jew who would skin a flea for a ha'penny'. Martha was a spinster with a deep, abiding distrust towards all men, while Anne was a widow, and, according to her account, was still fond of the opposite sex. When relations between the two were very strained, they became 'Mrs Murphy' and 'Miss Gillespie' to each other. Anne turned round as Martha's substantial figure appeared in the doorway, and sniffed disdainfully. The cook was attired in a black bonnet and cloak, she wore the Pioneer temperance brooch, and looked the essence of virtuous respectability. She gave one comprehensive glance at Anne, and then looked rather severely at the two nurses seated so cosily at her kitchen table. Mary, who knew Martha's every mood, understood that she was not too pleased to see her kitchen occupied, and hastened to make amends.

'Well, Martha,' she said, 'I have been taking French leave you see! I do hope you won't mind?—just for tonight you know, and there's a nice cup of tea on the pot,' she added insinuatingly, 'perhaps you would like it?'

Here Anne sniffed more loudly than before.

Martha proceeded to untie her bonnet strings, remarking as she did so,

'Mrs Murphy seems in more need of the tea, Nurse, I think. She seems to have a bad cold all of a sudden, and it might do her good in another way too.'

This was said with a significance not lost on Anne, but totally ignored by that lady in her reply. 'You didn't lose your way tonight, I hope, cook' she said, in her most patronising manner, leaning rather heavily against the kitchen table as she spoke, 'city streets do be very confusing to country persons.' Martha made no reply, but walked placidly round putting things straight here and there, but Mary knew that she was 'nursing her wrath to keep it warm,' and accordingly was very anxious to get Anne off to bed before hostilities went further. This, however, was easy to wish, but hard to accomplish.

'Yes, indeed, poor country folks do be stupid when they come up to the city,' continued Anne; 'not that they're stupid in other ways though. Ah! no—not at all! Sure they'd take the bread out of a poor Dublin person's mouth any day—living on a ha'penny a day, and with their cheese-parin' and bone scrapin'.'

Here Martha's face became of a mottled hue, a danger signal, and Mary hastily threw herself into the breech.

'Oh, Anne,' she cried quickly, 'Nurse Ray's best boy is upstairs—Mr Kelly you know. I'm sure she would like you to see him.'

The sitting-room was at least on the way upstairs and if she got Anne thus far she might be able to manage her the rest of the journey to her bedroom, for Mary noticed that every moment was making her more intoxicated.

'Come, Nurse Maguire, and we'll all go upstairs,' she continued, and between the two nurses Anne was conducted to the upper regions, Martha gazing after them with cold contempt.

At the sitting-room door, however, Mrs Murphy became

suddenly shy and coquettish, until Daisy Ray, hearing the scuffling outside, came to the door and opened it. Then Anne advanced unsteadily but smilingly into the room and stood gazing benevolently at Brendan Kelly, who, half amused, half embarrassed, stood regarding her from a man's vantage ground—the hearthrug.

'Nurse Ray's young man—I see,' said Anne. 'Yes, just so! Ah, well, we were all young—yes, I say we were all young once! I remember when I ——'

Mary interposed here, not knowing what revelation might follow.

'Anne! I want you upstairs—for a *special* purpose!' and the handmaid allowed herself to be led out of the room. But once outside she insisted on returning to give the young couple her blessing, and again, and yet again was the performance repeated until Mary losing patience, literally ran her upstairs and into her bedroom where, after removing her candle and matches, she shut the door, which had a convenient bolt on the outside.

Then with a sigh of relief, she went downstairs, knowing that Anne would now retire quietly.

'Yes, she's a protégé of Mac's,' Daisy was telling the others when she returned to the sitting-room, 'she got Matron to take her on here, and is always trying to reform her! Sometimes she will keep sober for months together, but then again we never know when she will go off on a burst like this! I really don't know why Mary bothers with her.'

'Because I like her!' said Mary, promptly. 'I don't know how it is, but I would rather have Anne with all her failings and backslidings than the sober, respectable Martha, who always seems to me such a typical old Pharisee!'

'Ah, well, Mac—you always had a fondness for the black sheep!' said Daisy, which statement was perfectly true.

Shortly afterwards the two visitors left St Columba's, and the nurses went up to bed—Mary not forgetting to give a look into Anne's room in passing. The innocent one, partially disrobed, lay on the bed in a deep and noisy slumber.

'Patient breathing heavily!' Mary reported with a laugh, as she rejoined Daisy, closing Anne's door behind her, but leaving it unlocked this time.

Mary Carmichael slept very restlessly, and heard all the fuss and noise of the others returning from the dance about four o'clock.

She sighed as she turned her pillow in a vain effort to court slumber, and yet why she sighed she could not have said.

Of course she and Daisy were the only ones at early Mass that morning, and very bare and cold the breakfast table seemed on their return.

'The others have leave to stay in bed till ten o'clock,' said Nurse Ray as she cut some bread. 'Mac! *do*, like an angel, stir the pot *well!*—I don't care whether it's vulgar or not—and give me a decent cup of tea for once!'

'That's just what I'm going to do,' said Mary, 'and I'm going to run up with a cup to Nurse Seeley—I promised her that I would.'

'Very well,' replied Daisy, 'but don't stay gossiping, Mac! It's not often that you have the chance of enjoying a cup of tea yourself in the morning—so hurry back! You'll have plenty of time for talking after dinner.'

'All right!' sang out Mary gaily, as she place two cups, the teapot, and some bread and butter on a tray and left the room.

Nurse Seeley shared her room with Nurse Lenehan, one of Mary's pet aversions, but greatly as she disliked the girl, Mary Carmichael was not small natured enough to leave her without tea when she was bringing it to her room-mate. She tapped lightly on the door, and turning the handle, entered, looking round rather helplessly for somewhere to deposit her laden tray. The dressing table was a confused medley of combs, brushes, ribbons, laces, gloves, powder puffs and a score of other frivolities, while the top of the chest of drawers was similarly littered, and the two chairs which the room contained were heaped with the discarded evening gowns—even the floor was strewn with slippers and stockings, handkerchiefs and a few withered flowers.

Mary gave a little chuckle as she surveyed the scene. 'Now, then, you two!' she cried. 'What about a cup of tea?'

Nurse Seeley stirred and yawned, then as she saw Mary pouring out the tea, she gave a sigh of contentment.

'Oh! Mary, you jewel!' she said, 'I was just parched! You know, I never sleep much after a dance.'

Her lovely dark hair was loose on the pillow, for she had taken out the pins and not troubled to comb or plait it, so tired had she been on her return from the dance; the sleep was still heavy in her eyes and her moulded arms showed prettily from the short sleeves of her lacy night-dress. Mary thought what a pretty picture she made as she handed her the tea.

'Well, and how did you enjoy yourself?' she asked; 'but, indeed, Seeley, I'm sure *you* had a good time anyway—you always do!'

'Oh, yes, it was all right. There was quite a decent crowd there, and everything went A1,' replied Nurse Seeley; and Mary, with half envious sigh, which in spite of all her good resolves she could not utterly repress, turned cup in hand to the other bed.

Here a very different picture met her view. Nurse Lenehan was a plain, sallow featured young woman, whose very scanty locks, of a nondescript yellow hue were tightly screwed up in hair curlers. She wore a severely useful flannelette night-dress, and her small foxy eyes surveyed Mary with a malicious gleam, even as she took the welcome cup from her.

'You should have been there anyway, Miss Carmichael,' she said, with a keen note of enjoyment in her voice. 'I can tell you that Dr Delaney had a good time there. He danced four or five times with Nurse Ormsby—everyone remarked it. But don't go and get jealous now!' She finished with an unkind little laugh.

Mary had turned her back and professed to be occupied with the breakfast tray, but the hands fumbling amongst the plates were not very steady. The she heard Nurse Seeley laugh and say gaily, 'Yes, Mac, dear, Theo was there. But he didn't come especially to the dance—some medical club to which he belongs gave a St Patrick's night dinner at the Gresham, and he just looked into the ballroom afterwards to see what was going on.'

'Just looked in?' repeated Nurse Lenehan spitefully; 'Well! his looking in took up a couple of hours anyway! And he spent most of the time looking at Nurse Ormsby, if you ask me!'

But by this time Mary Carmichael was herself again and she laughed in her own gay fashion as she answered: 'My dear Nurse! Surely you don't think that I begrudge the poor man a few hours' pleasure, do you?—even if it is spent away from my very charming society! And as for Julie Ormsby, she's a dear, and lovely too, and I wouldn't wonder at Theo or any other man dancing as often as he could with her! Don't you know that she is one of my own particular pals, and if I was a mere man I would have run away with her ages ago!'

Nurse Lenehan looked rather shamefaced, while Nurse Seeley laughed.

'You were always crazy over Nurse Ormsby's looks, Mac,' she said, 'but do you know she didn't look as pretty as usual last night!'

'Oh, well, she couldn't look plain if she tried,' said Mary. 'No more tea, ladies? No? All right then, I must run off now—duty calls you know,' and she went downstairs humming gaily to herself. But although she had shown such a brave front to the others and laughed matters off, still in her heart of hearts Mary Carmichael was a little sick and sore at the thought that Theodore Delaney should have gone to the nurses' dance without her. He knew quite well that she would not be there, and it would have been quite as easy for him to have gone straight home after dinner as it was for him to 'stroll' into the ballroom, even if it was only for a look round. And as for Julie Ormsby—well, he needn't have danced four times with her anyway! And for the first time since she had known Dr Delaney, Mary Carmichael felt a sharp pang of jealousy stabbing her to the very heart.

She dressed and went out on her rounds, and she had finished her first few cases before she began to feel 'normal' again. Then just as she was beginning to take a more cheerful view of the matter she almost ran into the arms of Mary Blake as she turned a corner with her mind far away. Two laughing exclamations sounded simultaneously, and then Mary Carmichael said, 'Oh! Mary, I was just thinking of you! Do come along and let us have tea somewhere. I do so want to talk to you!'

And over their tea and scones Mary Blake listened to her friend's tale of woe.

At its close she laughed heartily.

'Well! Mary Carmichael!' she said then, 'I wonder—I do wonder at you! But I suppose all things must be forgiven to the victims of the tender passion!'

Then as the other Mary flushed and looked almost offended, she leaned forward and laid her hand on hers.

'My dear!' she said softly, 'don't—don't be foolish! Don't you know Theodore Delaney even yet? Why you should know him better than anyone else, and yet you are doubting him!—actually doubting his faith and honour! Why dear old girl, haven't you realised that in Theodore Delaney you have an honourable, truthful gentleman—one who could never stoop to deceive a woman in anyway—especially the woman he cares for!'

Mary Carmichael smiled across the table through a mist of tears.

'Oh, Mary,' she sighed, 'I am a wretch. Of course I know that Theo is all you say and more, but—but just for the moment——'

'Just for the moment you felt horribly jealous—and of your own special friend too! I'm ashamed of you!' and Mary Blake laughed at her friend's discomforted face.

'Oh! Mary, don't, like a dear, tease me any more! But, tell me now, how you are all at home, and how is Clare?'

And so the subject was changed and the two friends chatted away on various other matters as they finished their tea. And Mary Carmichael kneeling later on before the Tabernacle wept tears of remorse that she should ever have doubted, even for one moment, the unsullied truth and honour of he who was her king amongst men.

Holy week came and the Catholic Church entered upon her days of fasting and penitence—of prayers and ceremonies. Clare Castlemaine went with her cousins to see some of the Altars of Repose in the city churches, and in one of them she saw Mary Carmichael. She was kneeling a little way off, her eyes were fixed on the altar and her lips moved in silent prayer. Clare watched her curiously, and thought she looked pale and thin.

'Killing herself fasting, I suppose!' she said to herself. 'Oh, dear! what a strange religion it is altogether, and yet what an extraordinary hold it has over the people!' She gazed around the church, noting the ever shifting crowd of worshippers passing and repassing towards the Altar of Repose, ablaze with lights and fragrant with flowers.

The Blakes went from church to church, untiring and untired, until poor Clare felt that she should faint from exhaustion, and the day, too, was very warm and oppressive for the time of year. And yet, as she reminded herself several times, she was not even fasting, and for the last few days she knew well that a very real abstinence—with the exception of herself—had been observed in the Blake household.

It was Shamus who notice her pale face presently.

'You look just done up, Clare—I vote you and I make tracks for home! I can finish my visits in the evening.'

'Oh, don't bother coming with me—please!' cried Clare. 'I am tired, but I can easily get home by myself. And you—if you have more churches to visit—oh, get them over now for you must be dead beat!'

But a gay laugh was the only reply, as Shamus piloted her towards a passing tram.

Two years later Clare Castlemaine recalled the sunny afternoon of that Holy Thursday, and saw again through a veil of burning tears the handsome face of Shamus Blake, and seemed to hear again his gay and tender voice.

Good Friday dawned, and Dublin's Catholic thousands fasted and mourned, and the churches were crowded with worshippers from morn till night. And Clare Castlemaine, stumbling to her seat in what appeared to her almost terrifying darkness as she went with Tom and Shamus to the Three Hours, found herself wondering again over this strange and mystical, yet wonderfully living Faith.

And on Good Friday night Mary Carmichael stood, pencil in hand, and drew it through the last day of her self-imposed penance.

'Tomorrow! Tomorrow!' she breathed to herself with shining eyes. 'Oh! I cannot believe it! To think that at last I can count the very *hours!* and not so long ago it was weeks—then days, and now—*now* it is only hours! Oh! for nine o'clock tomorrow morning! I do hope there won't be many other rings at the 'phone just then, for I will be thinking that each one is *the* ring! Oh! I hope I'll go to sleep at once, so that the morning will come the more quickly.'

Needless to say this is what she did not do, for it is indeed a mere truism that the more we woo Morpheus the further he flies from us, and the other way about. So she tossed and turned for hours, going over and over in her imagination the meeting with Dr Delaney the following evening—what *he* would say and what *she* would say—whether he would admire her new coat and tricky little velvet cap which every one said suited her so well, but which he had not seen yet. And she wondered would he tell her how he had missed her, and wondered too which of them had felt the separation most.

But at last her tired brain composed itself, and Mary Carmichael fell asleep.

Breakfast the next morning was like a dream to her. This meal was generally finished by half-past eight—it was short if not sweet but this morning it seemed to Mary an almost interminable repast. How the nurses did dawdle! Would Nurse Lenehan never finish that third piece of bread and butter! And then Matron, who usually had little to say at the first meal of the day, became quite chatty, meandering along about some meeting at the Mansion House to which she had been a few days ago.

But at last—at last it was over, and Mary free to race upstairs. She had decided to dress at once in her outdoor uniform and be ready to leave the Home for her work as soon as her chat at the 'phone was over—for that would certainly take a little time. Oh! but the sound of his voice over the wire would be music in her ears! It was only now—now when her penance was over and she was to meet him and talk to him as of yore—that Mary realised how hungry she was for the sight of his face and the sound of his dear voice.

She was pinning on her bonnet when Daisy Ray entered the room with some letters in her hand.

'Here is your post, Mac,' she said. 'It was late this morning. I'll leave them on the bed here for you as Matron wants me in the office.'

'All serene!' cried Mary gaily, and having arranged her bonnet to her satisfaction she turned to look at her letters.

Two from the Blakes—she recognised Angel's scrawl and Mary's neat calligraphy; three from nurse friends in London, probably with Easter wishes, and then—then one in his familiar handwriting.

Before she opened it some feeling of coming sorrow gripped her heart. A moment she stood rigid, looking at the envelope in her hand, then dropping the others anywhere on the floor, Mary sat down on the bed and opened Dr Delaney's letter.

And this is what she read:—

'Dear Miss Carmichael,

How are you these times? It seems ages since we met, and I do hope that you are as fit as ever, and have not been overworking yourself. I suppose you expected a call over the 'phone this morning? However, I am writing instead, as, for various reasons I think it better. I am afraid I will not be able to arrange a meeting with you for this evening, as I am exceptionally busy at present; but, doubtless we shall meet somewhere before long.

With kind regards and all good wishes for Eastertide.

I am,

Very faithfully yours,

Theodore J. Delaney.'

Outside in the city square cars and taxis were rushing past, and the noise of the trams sounded every few minutes. Through St Columba's itself doors banged and nurses called to each other as they got ready for the morning's work. But inside the bedroom was a dead silence—the woman on the bed sat rigid and still with the letter clasped tightly in her hand. Fully ten minutes were ticked away by the little clock on the mantelpiece and then the silence was broken by a stifled moan, and Mary Carmichael lay prone, her hands clutching the bedclothes in agony, her eyes wide open and terror-stricken.

Two inquisitive city sparrows hopped on the windowsill and looked curiously into the room, but the next minute they flew away again. They had not liked the picture they had seen there—and yet it was an everyday occurrence—only a woman passing through her Gethsemane, and treading it—as we all must tread it—alone.

CHAPTER XI

ONE DAY IN A WOMAN'S LIFE

It was nine o'clock on Easter Sunday morning, and the Blake family, having all returned from early Mass, were assembled around the breakfast table. Bride was absent, as she always helped at one of the Free Breakfasts on Sunday morning, and having been at seven o'clock Mass she had rushed home for a cup of tea and then was off to that part of the city where the breakfast for the poor was given. She would be home again about half-past nine or a little later, for even on Sundays Bride lived the strenuous life, and indeed would not have been happy otherwise.

Clare Castlemaine had not gone to Mass with her cousins that morning. The services and ceremonies of Holy Week—to which she had gone more or less out of curiosity—had attracted her strangely, and almost alarmed at the effect which they had had upon her, she had made up her mind to go no more.

'Bride is not back yet, of course?' said Mary, as she poured out the tea. 'However,' glancing at the clock—'she won't be long. I hope she will remember to tell Mary Carmichael to be sure to come early tonight.' Mary Carmichael also helped at the Free Breakfasts in the same building as Bride, and the latter had promised to give her a message from Mary Blake.

'Talking of Mary Carmichael,' said Norah suddenly, 'I saw Dr Delaney last night when I was coming home from confession. And who do you think was with him?' There was a general laugh round the table, and more than one voice answered her gaily. 'Who! why Mary of course! Ask us another, Norah darling!'

'Wrong! Wrong! all of you!' responded that young lady. 'It wasn't Mary Carmichael at all that was with him!'

'Not Mary Carmichael?' repeated her eldest sister in rather puzzled tones. 'Who was it then, Norah? His mother or sister, I suppose?'

'No, then! 'Twas neither his mother nor his sister—or his aunt or cousin or any relative! It was Julie Ormsby, looking as pretty as a picture in a Christmas number—so there!' and Norah looked round the table, feeling rather proud to have been able to impart such unexpected information. There was a puzzled silence on the part of the others, and Mary and Tom especially looked bewildered and rather worried.

But Pat only laughed as he remarked:

'Well, if Dr Delaney happens to meet Julie Ormsby—or any other girl for the matter of that—going probably the same way as himself, is there any reason in the world why they shouldn't walk a few yards together? That is likely what happened. Oh! Norah, jewel, you have got a bee in your bonnet—or rather under that sweet little hat of yours!'

Before Norah could reply the door opened and Bride entered in her usual quick, alert manner. Drawing off her gloves she took her place at the breakfast table, remarking as she did so that she was rather later than usual on account of having such a big crowd for the Free Breakfast on that morning.

'Did you give Mary Carmichael my message?' asked Mary. 'She wasn't there,' was the reply. 'Never turned up, and that made us all doubly busy, for Mary is so good at the work that she is worth two of the others. I can't think what happened her, for she so seldom fails us, and she knew that we expected an extra crowd this morning. I certainly think she might have managed to come, and I shall tell her so tonight.'

But as it happened, Bride had no opportunity of doing so, for Mary Carmichael did not pay her promised visit to the Blake family that evening.

She had got through Saturday someway—how she hardly knew, and never afterwards could she remember much of that day. It was as though some other personality—some unknown being—had taken possession of her body and had gone round her district and dressed bad legs and sore fingers and burnt children, and had made old women's beds and all the rest of her morning's work. She came back at dinner time and sat through the meal—actually eating too, but what she was eating she neither knew nor cared. The other nurses noticed little except that she was pale and tired looking—stupid and heavy, but she said she had a headache and as she was subject to very bad ones this made a reasonable excuse.

Daisy Ray and Nurse Seeley were the only ones who knew that she expected to have met Dr Delaney that night, and as Mary passed through the hall on her way to the cloakroom after her evening visits, she met these two on the stairs.

'Hello, Mac!' called out Nurse Seeley gaily, 'feeling better, old girl? You must try and pull yourself together for this evening you know!'

Mary Carmichael stood for a moment looking at her in a stupid, rather vacant fashion.

'You poor thing!' said Daisy Ray tenderly. 'Your head must be very bad! How unfortunate you should have it *tonight!* How distressed Theo will be!'

Mary Carmichael moistened her dry lips as if she was going to speak, but did not do so, and after another half stupid, half puzzled look at her two friends, she passed slowly up the stairs, leaning heavily on the bannisters.

'What is the matter with Mac?' asked Daisy Ray, 'she looks so queer. I never saw her like that before.'

'Nor I,' replied the other. 'Her head must be really bad—she looks like one who is stupefied with pain,' which was true, but not in the sense that Nurse Seeley meant. Indeed it is very probable that if Mary Carmichael had had to undergo very severe physical pain on that night she would hardly have felt it, for she was benumbed in body and soul—dead spiritually and mentally, and she seemed incapable of physical feeling.

She did not appear at supper, and when Daisy Ray came up afterwards with a cup of tea, she found Mary seated at the open window gazing down—but with unseeing eyes—at the busy Square beneath.

'Are you no better, dear?' asked Daisy. 'Here's a cup of tea, try and take it and a biscuit. Have you taken anything for your head? You know it's after eight—don't you want to go out soon?'

Mary Carmichael took the cup of tea in her hand, but made no effort to drink it.

Daisy began to feel rather frightened about her friend's condition. Could she be going to be really ill?

'Mac, dearest!' she said, 'do you feel bad?—is the head very painful? Do speak, old girl, and tell me how you feel.' Mary Carmichael looked at her then.

'How do I feel?' she repeated slowly; 'I don't feel at all, Daisy dear—I can't feel.'

'Well, drink your tea!' urged Daisy still anxiously.

Mary drank the tea obediently, and eat the biscuits; then she brushed the crumbs off her apron and handed the cup back.

'And now won't you dress?' said Daisy. 'You will be awfully late dear for your appointment.'

Mary turned and looked at her.

'What appointment?' she asked quietly.

'What appointment?' repeated Daisy Ray, incredulously. 'What appointment! Good heavens, Mac, why, I mean your meeting with Dr Delaney, of course.'

The other continued to look at her for a moment in silence, then—

'Dr Delaney?' she repeated slowly. 'I don't know him.' Daisy Ray stood as one petrified—she looked an almost absurd picture of bewildered consternation as she stared, tea-cup in hand, at the quiet figure by the window. Then her nurse's training came to her aid. She saw and recognised at once by the clue just given to her that the other was suffering from some great shock, and all Daisy's professional instincts came uppermost. She placed the cup and saucer on the table and moved over to the window.

'It's getting quite chilly, Mac,' she said composedly. 'I think we will shut down this window—at the bottom anyway—its open enough at the top to give us air. And now come and I'll help you to undress—you know your head won't get better until you have had a sleep.'

And Mary obeyed her like a child, allowing Daisy to take off her clothes, and settle her comfortably in bed. 'And now I'm going to fill a hot jar for your feet, dearie,' she said, and left the room. But once outside the door she caught her breath with a little dry sob, and ran downstairs with white cheeks and anxious eyes, and opening the door of the Recreation room she beckoned to Nurse Seeley, and almost pulled her into the cloakroom.There was no one in it, and Daisy switching up the light, turned and confronted her friend.

'Good heavens, Daisy; what's the matter?' exclaimed Nurse Seeley.

'Oh, Seeley; oh, Seeley,' was all the affectionate little thing could say.

'Daisy! what is it?'

'Oh, Seeley, it's Mac!—it's dear old Mac!'—and fighting hard with the sobs that threatened to overwhelm her Daisy Ray told of her interview with Mary. The other listened horror-stricken.

'Oh! my God!' she said, adding almost in a whisper, 'it will kill her—Oh! Daisy, it will kill her!'

Anxiously they conferred together, but they knew that there was nothing for them to do that night.

'Oh, how could he! how could he?' said Daisy. 'Oh, Seeley; would you ever have believed it of Dr Delaney?'

'Never!' replied the other, 'Never! I simply can't realise it. Oh, poor old Mac! How will she ever get over it?'

They took the hot jar upstairs together, and by a great effort forced themselves to talk quietly and unconcernedly to that silent, unresponsive figure lying on the bed and staring at the wall with wide, open eyes.

And so Mary Carmichael passed the hours of Easter eve—that Easter Eve to which she had been looking forward for long weeks, counting the very days and hours. And so she lay wide eyed and sleepless through the long, long night. Daisy Ray had prevailed on Nurse Johnson to change beds with her and let her sleep in Mary's room, explaining that she was anxious about her as she seemed so ill. And Daisy had kept awake for several hours, but at last, almost against her will, she had dropped off to sleep. As the hours went by Mary Carmichael seemed to pass out of the dull lethargic state in which she had been all that day, and in doing so she began to realise more distinctly what this terrible thing was that had come upon her like a veritable bolt from the blue, shattering in one awful moment all her dreams and hopes, all her happiness and joy. And yet even as she began to realise it, her poor brain was thinking over and over again—'Can it be true? Can it be true? Is this real or am I dreaming?' She would put her hand to her head and push back her heavy hair with a helpless puzzled gesture, and again she would ask herself, 'Can it be true?' But at last she found herself forced to answer back—'Yes, it is true—quite true!' And then indeed the iron entered into her soul, and Mary Carmichael lying quiet and still, never even moving for fear of disturbing Daisy, suffered such tortures, such mental and spiritual anguish, that the memory of that night will never pass from her—never be erased from her heart for the very thought of it years afterwards was like a knife turning slowly in an unhealed wound.

Early in the morning the bells for first Mass awakened Daisy Ray. Opening her eyes she was puzzled for the moment to find that she was not in her own bed, and then in a flash everything came back to her. She glanced swiftly towards Mary, but could not see her face, which was turned from her. 'Mac!' she called softly, 'are you awake, dear?'

'Yes.'

'How are you feeling? Is your head easier?' For Daisy thought it better to keep up the fiction of the bad headache—'and probably she had a headache too, poor thing!' she thought.

'My head is all right, thank you,' was the quiet answer.

'I suppose you don't feel able to go to early Mass?' enquired Daisy, as she drew on her stockings.

'I am not going to Mass.'

'Well, I think you are wise, dear, to take a rest. A late Mass will be best for you this morning.'

There was no reply, and Daisy Ray went on with her toilet, vaguely uneasy in her mind.

When she was finished and ready to go out, she went and stood beside Mary's bed for a moment.

'I'll bring you up a cup of tea, Mac,' she said softly, 'when I come back. Just lie quiet and rest until you feel better.' Then she went down to the landing below and knocked at Nurse Seeley's door.

'All right—one moment,' came the reply, and almost immediately afterwards the door opened and Nurse Seeley appeared ready for Mass too.

'How is Mac?' were her first words.

'Just the same, I think,' was Daisy's reply, 'she lies there like a log, and seems to take no interest in anything. Oh! Seeley, don't forget her in your prayers for I'm terribly anxious about her.'

On their return they ventured down to the kitchen. Martha was still absent at Mass, but Anne—a regenerated, spotless Anne—arranged a dainty little tray with tea and bread and butter for her beloved Nurse Carmichael. Together the two friends carried it up the weary flights of stairs and knocked at the door.

'Come in,' and Mary's tones were composed and indifferent. She turned and looked at them as they entered, but it was almost the look that she would have given to strangers.

'We have brought you some tea, Mac,' said Nurse Seeley, because poor Daisy, feeling a sudden lump in her throat had gone over to the window apparently to adjust the blind.

'And how are you today?—feeling better?'

'Thank you—that is kind of you. Yes, I'm quite well this morning—my head was rather bad last night, but it's all right now.'

She sat up and began to take the tea in a quiet, matter of fact manner. The other two were rather nonplussed. If only Mary had been more natural—more communicative, and inclined to take them into her confidence. They could not help feeling very curious as to what had taken place between Dr Delaney and herself, and they would certainly have welcomed any confidence that Mary might have given them, and nothing she said would have been repeated by either of them—both were too much attached to her to gossip over her private concerns.

But Mary Carmichael showed not the slightest inclination to impart any information on the subject over which they were puzzling her brains. On the contrary, she seemed not to grasp that there was anything to be spoken about out of the ordinary.

She finished her tea composedly, and handed the tray to Daisy with a smile of thanks.

'And now I think I must get up,' she said.

'I suppose you will get eleven Mass, or will you wait for twelve? But I am afraid the last would be too long for you today,' said Nurse Seeley.

'I don't know—I haven't thought about the matter,' and again the cold indifference of her voice struck the others unpleasantly.

'Well, we will leave you now to dress,' they said, and went down the stairs together, feeling strangely depressed.

Both had engagements with friends for the evening, but they had some cases to see during the morning, and promising to themselves to see Mary again at the early dinner, they went about their work.

Left to herself, Mary dressed leisurely and quietly. When she was doing her hair before the mirror she looked at her reflection in some surprise. Truth to tell, she hardly recognised herself as the same person who had gazed into the mirror yesterday morning with red cheeks and shining eyes—eyes soft with loving expectancy. The face that looked back at her now from the glass was haggard and pale, the eyes dull with a hard look in their depths. She looked many years older, for lines and wrinkles were there which surely were not visible yesterday morning. Yesterday! Was it really yesterday—or a hundred years ago?

She was off duty today, but she dressed in uniform and slipping on her bonnet and cloak went down the long stairs and across the wide hall without seeing anyone. She opened the hall door and passed out into the square, walked rapidly in the direction of Nelson's Pillar.

The streets were very full this Easter Sunday with crowds coming from and going to the various Masses, and others, their religious duties over, setting off for a day's pleasure in the country or seaside.

Mary mounted to the top of a Dalkey tram, and in a few minutes she was leaving the city behind her. She realised now for the first time how anxious she had been to get away somewhere—anywhere, but out of sight and sound of St Columba's, and all connected with it. Even Nurse Seeley and Daisy Ray were unbearable to her now. She must get away somewhere and think—*think* —what was to be done—for that she could continue in her present position she knew was impossible. Both she and Dr Delaney had been so well known in their own social circle and had had so many mutual friends—all of whom she knew had considered their engagement as practically settled—that for Mary to stay in Dublin and face the gossip, the smiles, and shrugs that her fancy conjured up, would be impossible to one of her temperament. Already she could almost hear Nurse Lenehan's sarcastic comments, and see her mocking smile, and the pity and compassion of her real friends would be almost worse to bear.

There was only one thing to do, one course to follow and that was to get a transfer to a district in the country where she would be miles and miles from all those who knew of her humiliation. And before Blackrock was reached, Mary's mind was made up and she decided to see the Superintendent on the following day and to apply for a transfer. She smiled grimly at the thought of what her sensations would have been a few days ago if anyone had suggested such a thing to her. A country district! To Mary's city-bred mind the idea called up visions of muddy roads and thick boots, tramps over bogs and hills, wind and rain and discomforts innumerable. It meant too, narrow minded gossip instead of intellectual companionship, and long, lonely evenings—no more dances, theatres, lectures or concerts. She would have scorned the bare idea of such an existence—but now she contemplated it quietly, nay eagerly. She cared not where she went—she would have gone to Timbuctoo or the North Pole—the Sahara Desert—to anywhere, to any place where she would be unknown, and above all where she would not meet *him* . The bare thought that she might meet him suddenly—see him face to face again, made her almost faint.

She left the tram just before it reached Dalkey and proceeded to walk the rest of the way, passing through the quiet little town and going on towards Loretto. Just in front of her a nursemaid was wheeling a go-cart in which was sitting a charming wee maid of about two years old. She wore a white furry coat and her golden curls peeped beneath her sweet little bonnet. Mary looked at her and then—for all children loved Mary instinctively—the little one smiled and stretched out her hands in frank friendliness. But to Mary the baby smile was like a knife thrust reaching to her very heart, all the mother hunger within her cried out in pain and she almost moaned aloud in her anguish. Her mental sufferings were plainly written on her always expressive face, and the child—used to loving looks from those around her—became suddenly alarmed at the hard, white face looking back at her, and began to cry in a frightened way.

Passing Loretto, Mary went on in the Killiney direction until she found a quiet spot by the sea, where she sat down. It was one o'clock now—only one! she thought, gazing at her wristlet watch. Oh! what a long, long morning it seemed—that long night and long morning were stamped on Mary Carmichael's brain for all time. Here the beauty of Nature was all around, the silver sea shone at her feet, behind her were the woods and Obelisk of fair Killiney—and peace reigned everywhere save in one woman's unquiet heart.

She stayed here motionless, gazing blindly at the sea—and then walked back to Dalkey where she got some tea, as she felt very thirsty, but she could eat nothing. And so Mary Carmichael spent the hours of her Easter morning. No Holy Communion, no Mass, no prayers—spiritually she was dead. She knew it herself, and it did not seem to affect her in the least. Dr Delaney had been her type of a perfect Catholic, and he had acted as no man with a spark of honour or chivalry could act, he had left her broken and desolate—and yet he was considered by all who knew him to be a deeply religious man. Of what value was such religion then when one who professed it could act so? And again she had given up all intercourse with him during Lent as a penance, a voluntary act of self-denial to show her love and gratitude to God. And what was the result? This—this overwhelming blow, this desolation of body and soul. God had flung her gift back in her face and would have none of it—to Mary He seemed to say: 'You offered me a paltry six weeks of self-denial—I don't want it; but I will make your whole life now one long misery!'

'Religion!' said Mary Carmichael, in bitterness of spirit, 'prayers, fasting, self-denial! All shadows—shibboleths—lies!'

After she had finished her tea she walked to Kingstown, and sat on the rocks by the pier, gazing out across the Irish sea with hard, miserable eyes, that saw nothing of the beauty around her. She was not conscious of feeling tired for walking seemed to ease her mind in some degree, and just as people in physical pain often find relief in such exercise, so now she found it of help to her in her mental distress. About six o'clock she left Kingstown and started to walk back to town, but at Blackrock she became suddenly conscious of her sore and blistered feet, and entered a passing tram. As the evening was getting chilly she went inside. The car was fairly crowded, but Mary noticed none of the passengers except one lady who got in at Merrion. At first Mary only observed a slight and apparently girlish figure attired in the latest fashion. A stylish hat crowned an elaborate golden coiffure, and the face beneath the veil seemed to be one of milk and roses. The little bit of fuss she made as she entered the car and took her seat, glancing around her in a self-conscious way as she did so, attracted Mary's attention as she gazed at her idly. Just then the lady turned and looked sideways out of the window, and Mary noticed the perfect network of wrinkles—especially in the lower part of the face and neck—which were then revealed.

In spite of herself Mary continued to look more closely at her and the longer she looked, the older and older the lady seemed to become. The hair was a palpable wig, the 'milk and roses' enamel and rouge, and the figure pads and a good corset. It was not that she was merely middle-aged and endeavouring to take a few years from her age. No, the woman was really old.

'Sixty at least,' Mary found herself thinking.

She was indeed a very caricature of a woman—a grotesque figure—and yet oddly pathetic. One evidently who had missed all that she most desired in life and now when one would think that life for her was practically over and done with—she was still clinging to it, and trying pitifully to cheat the years that had passed over her head.

To Mary Carmichael, gazing at her with miserable eyes, she seemed like some horrid nightmare of which she could not rid herself—a veritable death's head, fashionably dressed, and sitting in mockery grinning at her across the tram. And into Mary's poor tortured brain came the questioning thought—'Will I be like her in the years to come? the bare, long, lonely years that lie before me.

Will I get older and older, and will I try and pretend all the time that I'm still young? Will I paint and powder and wear somebody else's hair? Oh! I wonder will I?'

It showed how distorted her mind was at the moment that such ideas should come to her. How the other Mary Carmichael—the cheerful, sane Mary—would have scoffed at the bare notion of such a thing! That other Mary would have looked at the poor creature opposite half in pity, half in amusement, sighed that any woman could make such a caricature of herself, and then would probably have shrugged her shoulders and thought no more of the matter. But the Mary of today—the tortured, wretched woman who had just found all her world tumbling down like a house of cards—that Mary could see only the tragedy of that unreal figure opposite and could only shudder in fear lest the future would turn her too into such another picture. The lady got out at Merrion Square—throwing 'the glad eye' even at the amused conductor as she daintily tripped down the steps.

Mary went on to the Pillar, and then walked to Dorset Street and entered the hall of a large tenement house of the decent sort. She went up the stairs and knocked at a door on the 'drawing-room' landing which was opened almost immediately by a stout motherly woman of about fifty, whose good-natured face lighted up on seeing who was her visitor.

'Why, it's Miss Mary!' she cried. 'Come in, Miss, dear. This is a pleasure to see you—and on Easter Sunday, too!' Mary followed her silently into the large bright living room. It was like most of the rooms one finds in the superior tenement class house. The boards were bare, but scrubbed very white; there was a dresser piled with delph, a cabinet piled with ornaments, a sofa, a couple of arm chairs, several kitchen ones and two little stools, and plenty of pictures mostly of religious or political subjects. A large fire was burning in the bright range and the table was set for tea. A man a few years the senior of the woman was sitting smoking, but on seeing Mary he took his pipe out of his mouth and rose to his feet. A baby—the woman's grand-child—was asleep in a cradle near the fire, and every detail of that poor room spelt the word—*Home.*

'Mark!' cried Kate Cassidy, 'Here's Miss Mary come to see us!' and she drew forward one of the armchairs. Then she seemed to notice Mary for the first time, her silence had puzzled her and she glanced at the girl's face. It was tired and haggard looking—years older, too, than the Mary who had sat in this room talking so gaily to her a few weeks ago—her visitor of tonight looked like a woman of forty or more.

Kate Cassidy had been Mary's nurse in the old days when James Carmichael and his pretty young wife had been alive, and she gazed now at the girl in pitiful dismay.

'Oh! Miss Mary, dear! what is it? Sure it's worn out and ill you must be! Sit down, darling; sit down and rest yourself.'

Mary looked up at the good motherly face bending over her, at the work-worn hands resting so tenderly on her shoulder, and then her glance wandered round the poor familiar room, at the cheerful tea table, at the man standing in the awkward manner of men when they feel they are not wanted—at the baby sleeping in its cradle. She looked at all first with hard unseeing eyes full of pain and misery—and then suddenly her frozen heart seemed to thaw, and she was only conscious of a terrible tiredness—of an aching heart hunger—of a great longing for sympathy, and she turned quickly and hid her face on the broad bosom where she had lain so often as a child.

'Oh! yes—yes! Kate!' she said brokenly, 'I am tired—so tired! Let me rest here—oh! don't sent me away! I'm so lonely and tired!—tired of everything!'

And so enfolded in Kate's strong arms, Mary at last gave way to nature's grief, and although her sobs were bitter at first, yet after a while the tears flowed easily until they fell like rain on her parched heart, and so gave her relief.

Exhausted at last she leant back in her chair, only a sobbing sigh escaping her now and then—like a tired child that sobs in its sleep.

Kate Cassidy, with rare tact, asked no questions as to what had upset her, but only inquired if she had been on duty that day, and if she had had her dinner, for the woman saw that Mary was really worn out.

'On duty?' repeated Mary dully, 'no, Kate, this was my Sunday off. I—I spent the day at Dalkey and Kingstown. I think—yes, I had a cup of tea at Dalkey—about half-past one I believe.'

'And now it's near eight!' exclaimed Kate; 'well, Miss Mary dear, 'tis no wonder you're tired out!'

She boiled the kettle and made the tea; she cut bread and butter and thin slices of boiled ham, and gently, tenderly, like a mother feeding her child, so she fed this nursling of hers. At first Mary thought that every mouthful would choke her, but presently Nature asserted itself, and she found herself eating and drinking and feeling the better for it.

At ten o'clock she was in bed in one of the little rooms off the living room—in bed and asleep—the sleep of utter exhaustion, physical and mental.

Then Kate Cassidy, wiping her eyes with her apron, went downstairs to find her 'old man,' who had taken refuge with neighbours in the 'parlour' below. She drew him outside and spoke.

'I don't know what's happened the child, Mark,' she said brokenly; 'some big sorrow it must be to have crushed all the life out of Miss Mary, and she so gay always.'

'No, she's not going back to the Home tonight—she's not able even to walk that short distance itself, and anyway she wants to stay here. So you go up to the Home and see the Matron or one of the nurses, and say that Miss Carmichael is not well, and is staying with me for the night.'

And so Mary Carmichael passed the hours of that Easter Sunday to which she had looked forward day after day during Lenten time.

CHAPTER XII

'UNDER WHICH KING?'

Three days had passed since Easter Sunday, and Mary Carmichael was still at Kate Cassidy's house. On Easter Monday she had been unable to leave her bed, tired out in body and mind, and so physically weak that it was an effort almost to lift her hand.

Daisy Ray and Nurse Seeley had called to see her early that day and were shocked at her appearance. They could hardly maintain their self-control before her, and both were glad to shorten their visit, for the sight of 'dear old Mac' once the life and soul of the Nurses' Home, now so weary and haggard with that dreadful stricken look upon her face almost completely unnerved them.

They reported to the Matron—for she was not one in whom they could confide or who would sympathise with any of her nurses sick or well—that Nurse Carmichael seemed very run-down and tired, and Miss McFarland—who had no use for a nurse who couldn't work and work hard—at once advised that Mary should apply for a holiday and return to her duties afterwards, when she felt quite well again.

So Mary was put off duty *pro tem*, with directions to report herself at the office of the Nursing Committee, when she would probably be granted a few weeks' leave of absence, and in a few days Mary called to see the Superintendent and applied not only for a temporary sick leave, but also for a transfer to a country district.

Miss Malcolm glanced keenly at her through her glasses. 'You want a transfer to the country, Nurse?' she said in surprised tones, 'but I always understood that you had a great objection to country districts, that you preferred the city in every way. Is this on account of your health?'

Her sharp eyes were scrutinising Mary all the time, thinking how really ill she looked, and wondering, but too tactful to question—what really was the matter with this nurse, one of the very best on her staff.

Meanwhile Mary was fighting hard for composure; she was frightfully nervous—why she hardly knew—and so weak in body and mind that it took all the will-power of which she was possessed to keep her from breaking down completely.

'Not altogether on account of my health, Miss Malcolm,' she faltered; 'but I—I think the country—the change would help me. Oh, please, Miss Malcolm, let me go, and soon.'

Miss Malcolm was a wise woman and recognised that this was no time for argument.

'Very well, Nurse,' she said quietly; 'there is a district vacant in the south-west —in Co. Clare. Will you take that?'

'Oh, yes, Miss Malcolm—anywhere,' was the reply, pitiful in its very eagerness.

And so matters were settled, and Mary Carmichael left the office with three weeks' sick leave granted to her, at the expiration of which time she was to report herself again and arrange finally for her transfer to the Co. Clare district.

She told Kate Cassidy languidly about these arrangements while that good woman was fussing around her with tea and toast.

'And I'm going to leave you too, Kate,' she said; and as her old nurse gave an exclamation of dismay, she went on—

'Yes, I know, Katie—and you have been a perfect dear to me—what I should have done without you I don't know—I daren't think of it. But now—well, somehow I have a wish to go out Ranelagh way. I know a decent old soul—she was a patient of mine once, with a room to let, and I'm going to take it for the three weeks.'

'God save us, Miss Mary, dear,' said Kate, 'and what would you do the likes of that for? And what about your friends, the Blakes? Sure they would be in a queer pucker if they knew you were in strange lodging, and them with their house always open to you as you know well.'

'Oh, yes, Kate—I know all that,' said the other, with the new note of utter weariness and indifference in her voice, to which Kate was now becoming accustomed.

'I know all that, but I—well, I'm going to Ranelagh, and that's all!'

And she went—without a word to any of her fellow-nurses, or to the Blakes, or indeed to anyone she knew. She did not even leave her address with Kate.

'The nurses would only be bothering you for it,' she said, 'and I want to be left in peace.'

In peace! alas! poor heart, peace was far from her yet. In after years Mary Carmichael used to look back with a sort of dull wonder at those days she spent by herself in Ranelagh. Wonder that she ever lived through them—or that in living she did not lose her reason. At times she very nearly did so, and then, when she was feeling really desperate she would go out and walk—walk—walk. She would sometimes leave the house about five or six o'clock and walk the roads and streets around until ten or eleven, trying to tire herself out so much that she might sleep at night. In vain. Tired in body she might be—aching in every muscle—but her brain knew no respite—ever active, ever working, it would go over and over again, the scenes of a few months past. Like a series of living pictures there would pass before her mental vision the hours she and Dr Delaney had spent together, their walks and talks, the picture houses they had frequented together, the theatres; and especially would she re-live, over and over again, the night they had seen the *Little King of Rome* on the film, and *Faust* at the Gaiety. The music of Goethe's masterpiece would ring in her ears until she would sit up in the bed, and in desperation put her hands over her ears as though the sound was material and she could thus shut it out, and in doing so also stifle the memories that were seared on her brain in red hot letters—never to be erased in this life. And all that time Mary never prayed, never entered a church.

The Blakes were greatly troubled about her, for ten days now they had not seen her or even heard about her. Inquiries at St Columba's and at Kate Cassidy's proved futile, no one knew where she had gone, or where she was staying.

Then one evening Bride announced, while taking her seat—late as usual—at the tea table: 'Oh, by the way, I saw Mary Carmichael today.'

'Where? When? How is she? What did she say? Why didn't she come to see us?'

A perfect tornado of questions poured forth upon her, for the whole family was present. Bride shrugged her shoulders. Of all the Blakes she was the only one who had not worried over Mary at this time, such a 'case' was not interesting from Bride's standpoint. Had Mary been in want or rags, a drunkard, a thief, or a girl of the streets—or even a respectable mother attending her Baby Club, then all Bride's sympathies would have been enlisted in her behalf, but as it was, she considered that her brothers and sisters were making too much fuss over this friend of theirs.

'I'm sorry to say that I can answer none of your questions,' she said. 'I was hurrying after Mrs Doyle, of whom I had just caught sight—that woman is really enough to dishearten anyone, promising to attend the Club regularly and then——'

'Oh, blow Mrs Doyle,' interposed Pat, 'get on Bride, do, and tell us about Mary.'

Bride stiffened at once. She was always a little difficult to get on with, as the others knew, and Mary Blake now interposed gently.

'Please, Bride, we are so anxious—tell us all you can.'

'Well, really, as I said, there is nothing to tell. I was hurrying after Mrs Doyle, and turning a corner I came face to face with Mary Carmichael. She was walking quickly and looking straight in front of her, but with the queerest expression, just as if she saw nothing. She didn't even see me, walked past me quite oblivious of my presence. Really, she might have been walking in her sleep for any notice she took of her surroundings.'

'But you stopped her? You spoke to her, Bride?'

It was Tom who spoke, and the anxiety of his voice made Bride turn and look at him rather curiously.

'Stop her?' she repeated, coldly; 'No, certainly not; I had my work to do, and if I had stopped then Mrs Doyle——'

'Oh, dash Mrs Doyle,' exclaimed Pat, and Shamus said something in Irish which seemed to relieve his feelings better than the mere Saxon tongue, to which poor Pat was restricted.

Mary and Tom left the dining-room together after tea was over, for they had promised to spend an hour with Angel, who was not so well these days. The child was fretting terribly over Mary's absence, for she was devotedly attached to her. By one accord they stopped in the hall and looked at one another. The haggard, anxious look on Tom's face went to Mary's heart and she slipped her hand through his arm as they slowly mounted the stairs together.

'Don't worry, dear,' she said gently. 'I know it's hard for you—but we—we can do nothing until we find where she is.'

'Oh, dear God!' said the other, 'If only anyone else but Bride had met her. What a piece of ill-luck!'

'Well perhaps it will be better luck next time,' said his sister, trying to cheer him, although her own heart was heavy within her.

On entering Angel's room they found that Clare was there before them. Angel raised herself eagerly on her couch when she saw them—she was literally trembling with eagerness, and a hectic flush burned on her cheeks.

'Oh, Tom! oh, Mary!' she cried. 'Clare has been telling me about

Bride meeting Mary Carmichael. Oh! why didn't she stop to speak!—why didn't she? How could she be so cruel as not to do so!'

'Hush, darling,' said Mary, putting her arms round the thin little form, 'It can't be helped now. Bride didn't think, you know—she was busy and worried over her cases.'

'Oh, bother her cases!' cried Angel, very much as her brother Pat had done; 'what are all her old cases beside my dear, dear Mary?'

Clare laughed, and even in Tom's sad eyes a ghost of a smile appeared. Angel was so seldom angry—it was such a rare occurrence, and alas, just now, so useless.

'Don't fret, sweetheart,' he said, stooping to stroke the soft fair hair; 'if Bride met her, she is still in Dublin, still near us, and surely one of the rest of us will meet her some day, and then we won't let her off so easily!'

'Oh, Tom!' said the little one piteously, 'I have had such awful dreams about Mary—and always, always she is standing on the brink of something—it's like a great rock or precipice—I don't know what, but she is standing there always and so near—*so near* to the edge. And oh, Tom, if you could see her face as I see it, night after night—night after night!'

They soothed her as best they could, those two who loved her so, and Clare Castlemaine stood and looked on. Since Mary Carmichael's trouble she had been going through a strange time, a time of storm and stress. In some queer inexplicable manner, Clare had always felt that her own life and future were bound up with Mary Carmichael, she had felt this ever since they had first met; particularly did she feel this in the case of religion. It seemed to Clare that the Catholic Faith, towards which she had been drawn almost in spite of herself during these last weeks, would stand or fall by the attitude that Mary would now adopt—by the spirit in which she would bear this trouble which had descended upon her with such overwhelming force. Nurse Seeley had come to see the Blakes, and knowing as she did, that they were such real friends of her dear Mac, she had confided fully in them and they now knew as much as herself. They talked over matters together, they planned and hoped and thought of this thing and that thing, but alas, what good could they do until Mary was found?

'Oh! I am afraid for her!' said Mary later on when only she and Tom and Clare were left talking downstairs, 'I am afraid for her.'

'You mean?' asked Tom, with the lines of pain showing more clearly on his honest face.

'I mean spiritually,' replied his sister.

Then she glanced rather wistfully at Clare.

'Perhaps I shouldn't speak of these things before you, Clare,' she said sadly; 'but I can't help it—my heart is sore tonight.'

'You see, Mary Carmichael is a convert, and a comparatively recent one, all zeal and fire and high ideals—like converts often are. But she is a queer mixture, and I'm so afraid that her religion may not stand this terrible strain that God has seen fit to put upon it—I'm so afraid that in sheer despair she may do something desperate.'

Clare looked up eagerly.

'That's just what I am interested in,' she said. 'I'll have a chance now to see what Catholics are made of, so to speak, to see what real good there is in their religion. If Mary Carmichael stands this test well and keeps her Faith as strongly as ever—well, then I shall know that there is something in that Faith—something worth living for, and worth dying for, too!'

Tom got up and, walking over to the fireplace, stood leaning against the mantelpiece looking down at her.

'Clare,' he said quietly, 'we are also wondering how Mary Carmichael will meet this trouble. Not, of course, that it would affect our Faith in anyway—that, thank God, is out of the question for us—but for her own sake we are terribly anxious. She is, as you know, a recent convert, very fiery and enthusiastic—apt in fact to run to extremes even in her religious duties, and for those very reasons we are somewhat afraid for her now.'

Clare listened eagerly.

'Oh, Tom,' she said, 'how do you think she will bear it?' Her cousin's face looked strangely haggard and drawn, as he replied briefly: 'God only knows!'

'You see, Clare,' said Mary, putting down her eternal darning for a few moments, and clasping her hands together in her lap, 'you see she idealised Dr Delaney so much, he was her type of perfect manhood—of truth and honour and chivalry, but above all of Catholicity at its highest and best. She looked up to him and regarded him as her ideal of Catholic manhood. She said to me: "In Theo I see what the Catholic Faith can make of a man."'

'Oh, that's nonsense,' said Clare, half angrily. 'I have met heaps of good men—honest and truthful, yes, and chivalrous, too. Men who would scorn to treat a woman as Dr Delaney has treated Mary Carmichael, and yet they hadn't any definite religious beliefs at all—much less were they Catholics.'

Mary Blake looked doubtful, but Tom said quietly, 'Yes, there are such men outside the Church; had they been within the fold they would probably have added to her army of saints.'

Clare smiled.

'Well, anyway,' she said, 'I'm going to wait and see how Mary Carmichael bears this trouble, which, of course, her Faith has taught her should be borne with Christian resignation.'

She left the room soon afterwards and Tom and Mary Blake were alone. Mary's eyes sought her brother's anxiously as he still stood on the hearthrug—his attitude moody and despondent. Lifting his head he caught Mary's glance, and forced a smile to his lips.

'Don't fret for me, sister mine,' he said in his quaint lovable way, and coming over to her he put his arms around her and leant his head on her shoulder; 'don't worry, sis; but pray for her—pray for her!'

'Oh, Tom, I do,' said Mary, the tears welling up to her eyes; 'If we could only see her, if we only knew more about the whole matter! I cannot think how Dr Delaney——' She stopped suddenly, for Tom had sprung upright, his hands clenched, and his eyes blazing.

'Don't, Mary—don't!' he said, in a choked voice; 'don't mention the villain's name for God's sake—for I cannot control myself when I think of him!'

His sister looked at him, half frightened—never had she seen this quiet, serious, and even-tempered brother of hers so aroused.

'Very well, dear,' she said gently, and turned the conversation. Meanwhile the subject of their thoughts was leading her lonely and miserable life in Ranelagh. Mrs Doolan, an old patient, had been delighted to have Mary in her little 'bedsitting-room' on the ground floor, and was very kind to her; but Mary was incapable these days of feeling either kindness or unkindness. Her feelings seemed still quite benumbed. Two facts alone stood out clearly before her mental vision—first, that Theodore Delaney had cast her aside when tired of her, had treated her as he would treat a woman for whom he had no respect, and secondly, he was a Catholic, and considered by all as an example of what a practical good Catholic should be. Therefore, for Mary, the Catholic Faith had failed.

'By their fruits ye shall know them,' she repeated bitterly to herself, often and often during this desolate time, and desolate she was indeed, weary and lonely; she had deliberately shut out her God and turned her back on heaven and all spiritual consolations, and on Earth, with all its human joys and sympathies also. A soul in such a state is fit for the assaults of our spiritual foes, and the arch-enemy of the human race, perceiving that she stood alone and helpless, and unprotected, drew near, knowing that here would be an easy conquest—for we cannot fight without weapons; and, alas, Mary Carmichael had laid aside all her spiritual armour.

One morning, after a more than usual sleepless night, she went out about ten o'clock, and turned her steps city-wards. She would for once risk meeting any of her friends, for she was tired of the streets and roads round Ranelagh and thought a change of scene would be more cheerful. She turned into Stephen's Green and stood for a moment idly watching with indifferent eyes the wild fowl on the water.

'Little Mary Carmichael! or do my eyes deceive me?'

Mary turned swiftly at the sound of the man's voice beside her, and she looked at him stupidly for a second. As she did so her mind went swiftly back to her London life and especially to one summer's day at Richmond, one of her 'days off,' and not the only one which she had spent in the fascinating company of Dr Charles Raymond.

Charles Vere Raymond, M.B., F.R.C.S.,etc., was a man of about forty years of age. Tall, slight and clean shaven and faultlessly groomed and tailored as usual; he stood and looked keenly at Mary, through his inevitable eyeglass. He was a very clever surgeon, and many a critical 'case' had Mary nursed for him in the past. He had thought very highly of her talents in her profession, and as a woman she had always possessed a curious fascination for him. She had seemed so different from the other nurses in the West End Home, whom he knew, and with whom he had flirted and amused himself in his idle moments. There was always 'something' about Mary which had gained his respect, and Charles Raymond was not one who thought very highly of women as a rule. He was devoted to his profession but merely as a profession, and regarded it from a purely scientific point of view. In his leisure moments—which however were not many—he led the typical life of a London man about town, and enjoyed without scruple any pleasures that came in his way. For the rest he was an avowed atheist and, according to his belief, this life spelt Finis for us all.

Slowly Mary held out her hand, and he grasped it warmly.

'So it is little Mac,' he said laughingly; 'I was only wondering when I arrived here a few days ago for a short holiday, whether I should see you or not. But you are not looking well! Why, our grimy London must have agreed better with you than your own dear Dublin seems to have done.'

Mary winced as she tried to smile at him in the old gay manner.

'I—I have not been very well lately,' she said, 'and I am on sick leave just now—but I'll soon be all right again.'

'It's to be hoped so,' replied Dr Raymond cheerily. But he was not deceived; his professional glance was too keen to be taken in by any such excuses, and he realised that the woman beside him was suffering, and that her sufferings were more of the mind than the body, although, so closely are the two interwoven—as none know better than physicians—her bodily health was affected also in a lesser degree.

'Let us sit down here,' he said, as they came to a seat, 'and now tell me all your news since we met last—let me see how long ago?'

'Three years,' said Mary, with a tightening of the lips as she remembered all that those three years had brought to her.

'Three years,' echoed Charles Raymond. 'So it is. And yet in some ways it seems only like yesterday that we drove down to Richmond together. Do you remember, little girl?—and our dinner afterwards at the Star and Garter?—and the drive back by moonlight.'

Mary did not answer. The devil was beside her—very close, and his arguments were very specious. After all why shouldn't she enjoy herself—if she could in this world? Perhaps there was no other? How was she to know?—all the whole building of her temple of Faith has fallen down—collapsed and lay in ruins beside her. God did not want her. He had flung back the sacrifice she had offered to Him—had scorned her gift. That was, if God existed. Did He, she wondered? Anyway, He was not for her, and here beside her the World, the Flesh and the Devil, if there was such a person!—were calling to every bad instinct she possessed. Still, although Religion and Faith made no appeal to her now, yet the habits and training of the last few years clung to her still. She moved a little further away from the man beside her, and as she did so her angel guardian drew a little nearer to her. Dr Raymond only lifted his eyebrows and smiled. He did not attempt to come any closer—he merely waited.

Mary spoke then—coldly.

'I hope Mrs Raymond is quite well? I saw in the papers that she had been ill a few months ago.'

'My wife?' and Charles Raymond shrugged his shoulders with easy indifference. 'Oh, yes—she's all right. We don't see much of each other, you know, she goes her way and I go mine—suits both of us!'

Having gone through the form of marriage with a handsome society woman, many years his senior, for the sake of her money and the better social position she could give him, Dr Raymond thought no more of the matter—that marriage entailed any obligations on his part never entered his head.

He laughed now, and ventured to edge a little closer to the girl beside him. This time she did not resent it.

'But don't let us waste time discussing my domestic affairs,' he said lightly, 'tell me about yourself Mac? Is it true what I heard a short time ago that you had really joined the Catholic Church, and made a vow never to enjoy life again? I must say that you have the appearance of having been immured in some dark convent cell!'

The tones were light, but the eyes searching her downcast face were keen enough. Truth to tell she puzzled him. She was not the frank, open Mary Carmichael of the old days, the Mary who was ready for any fun and frolic, but who, with it all, could and did always maintain her self-respect.

This woman beside him was not open—some secret trouble was crushing her—and she seemed hard and reckless, as if she cared little what she did or what became of her. What then about her religious zeal of which some of the London nurses had been telling him?

Mary sat silent for a moment, idly raking the gravel with the toe of her shoe. Then she lifted her eyes and looked at him with a more reckless expression than he had ever seen in any of the old London days.

'Well, yes, it's true,' she said, 'or rather, it was true, for I think I have had enough of Catholics—they are hypocrites—teaching one thing, and practising another.'

Charles Raymond leant back in his seat and laughed. Here

indeed was a piece of luck. The Gods were kind, and he would not have such a dull holiday after all.

'Well, as for that, my dear girl,' he said cynically, 'as far as I could ever discover, all forms of so-called Christianity are alike. Why if any of their sects really lived up to their teaching the world would be a very different place, and there wouldn't be much room in it for such a hardened sinner as myself! However, don't bother your head any more about these religious people—let them please themselves and go their way—and we will go ours. Now I have only a few days to spend in Dublin. Let us make the most of it, shall we? as if we were back in London three years ago.'

For one moment Mary hesitated—and the cause of her hesitation was a wonder to herself. It was no last appeal to her better self by religion or faith or morality—these existed no longer for Mary. But the picture that made her pause for a moment before taking her downward step was that of a frail fair-haired girl lying on a couch, of blue eyes looking—oh, so anxiously into hers, and of a sweet beseeching voice that seemed to say over and over again: 'Oh, Mary! Mary! don't!'

Angrily she brushed the vision aside, and turned with a reckless laugh to the man at her side.

'All right,' she said, in the slang of past days, 'I'm on.'

'Good,' said Charles Raymond, with quiet satisfaction.

'Well what about this evening then?'

• • •

Tea was over at the Blakes, on the evening of the same day. Shamus and Norah had gone out and Bride also was away at one of her numerous Committee meetings, while Pat had gone to see a fellow-student on the same road. Only Mr Blake, Mary and Tom were in the dining-room.

Suddenly a piercing scream, followed by a voice calling, 'Mary! Mary!' in tones of agonised supplication were heard. The three sprang to their feet simultaneously, and all cried, 'Angel', as though in one voice.

Tom reached her room first, quickly followed by his sister and Mr Blake. Angel was sitting up in bed—she had been too weak the last few days to be allowed up—her fair hair tumbling over her shoulders, her eyes wide open in seeming terror, and her cheeks flushed. She held out her trembling hands to her brother and bending over her he held them to his breast, while he tried to soothe her.

'Angel, dearest! what is it? what has happened to you?' asked Mary, coming to her other side.

'Oh, it's Mary Carmichael! It's Mary Carmichael!' half sobbed the girl. 'She's in danger. I don't know from what—but she's in awful danger, and she wants me—she is calling to me to help her! Oh, what will I do! what will I do!'

'Hush, darling, hush,' said Mary anxiously. 'You will make yourself ill if you go on like this! As for Mary Carmichael, sure we are all troubled for her, but what can we do, when we don't know where she is?'

'She's in a great big room at dinner,' said the sick girl, more quietly, 'and there are a lot of other tables around, and people in evening dress dining—it looks like a hotel.'

'She is wearing her evening frock—the one she wore at the dance before Christmas—and there is a red rose in her hair.'

Mary smiled, but her voice was anxious as she tried to soothe her young sister.

'You have been dreaming, dearie,' she said softly; 'lie down now and rest—and don't worry any more. Mary is sure to be found some day soon.'

Angel turned impatiently from her.

'Oh, Tom,' she cried beseechingly, the tears streaming from her eyes, 'go and find her, go and find her. There is a man sitting opposite to her and talking to her, and I don't like him—I don't like him! And Mary wants me! She called for me, I tell you; she called for me!'

Tom put her back gently amongst her pillows.

'I am going now, Angel,' he said quietly, 'and if I have to search every hotel in Dublin, I'll find Mary Carmichael, and with God's help I'll bring her back to you tonight!'

'Oh, Tom—*thank you!* thank you!' and Angel smiled once more. 'Go now and don't delay a minute! Give me my rosary beads, Mary, and I'll pray for him all the time he is away.'

Outside Angel's door, Mary looked at her brother rather doubtfully. 'Are you really going on this wild goose chase, Tom,' she asked. 'It was surely only a dream that Angel had—is it worth while?'

'Any chance—no matter how slender it may seem—is worth trying,' said Tom quietly, 'and you know Mary—although we cannot explain it—still this is not the first time that Angel has had her 'visions' as she calls them—and they always proved more or less true.'

Mary still looked sceptical, but she only said, 'Well! do what you think best, dear—only don't be later than you can help coming home.'

Mr Blake had been standing quietly by, but as Tom turned to descend the stairs, he went after him and slipped something into his hand.

'Take a taxi, Tom,' he said quietly, 'it will make your search easier and quicker.'

'Thank you, sir,' said Tom gratefully, and he knew then that he had his father's sympathy.

Tom Blake's search was not long after all. At the third hotel he found them—and they were seated opposite to each other at a little round table, and Mary wore her evening frock, and there was a red rose in her hair—just as Angel had said.

Only for noticing these details, Tom would almost have passed her over without recognition—so greatly can expression and demeanour alter one. For this reckless woman with the hard look in her beautiful eyes, who sat with her elbows on the table flirting openly—defiantly, with her companion, bore indeed little resemblance to the sweet, modest Mary Carmichael of his thoughts and dreams. A glass of champagne—as yet untouched—was beside her plate, and they were evidently about half way through dinner, which meal, it seemed to Tom, Mary was forcing herself to eat.

His heart contracted within him, but he braced himself for the ordeal, and holding himself more erect than usual he approached their table.

After all, even in these days, an odd Sir Galahad, may still be found in our midst.

'Mary,' he said, quietly but distinctly.

Starting violently, and deadly pale, she turned swiftly in her chair and looked at him.

Charles Raymond raised his eyebrows superciliously, a cynical smile playing around his lips, as he watched the drama enacted before him—although in his eyes it was only a rather amusing comedy.

For a moment Mary could not speak. Then her face hardened and she pulled herself together.

'What is it?' she asked in tones of ice. 'What do you want?'

'Angel wants you, Mary,' said Tom, still quietly and gently.

'Angel!'—there was a swift change in her voice, a softening of the countenance—'Angel! Is she—ill?'

'She has not been able to leave her bed or some days,' Tom replied, his eyes resting sorrowfully on the pale troubled face of the woman who was so dear to him—and never more dear than now in this her great hour of need—'and tonight—tonight she wakened from a short sleep calling for you, and would not be quietened unless I promised to bring you to her.'

Mary looked bewildered, and Charles Raymond surveyed Tom through his eyeglass as though he were some unique specimen of humanity. He was far from pleased at this interruption—he did not dream it would go beyond that—but although his gaze at Tom was insolent in the extreme, yet he could not help—from a medical standpoint—admiring the perfect physique, the fearless eyes, and the honest, open face of the man before him. He saw too few of this type in his beloved London.

'Might one inquire how this gentleman became aware of the fact that you were dining here tonight?' he asked of Mary sarcastically.

Mary started as though it had only occurred to her now to wonder how Tom knew where to come. She turned her inquiring gaze on him now.

'Yes!—how did you know?' she asked, with some eagerness. 'Angel told me,' replied Tom quietly, 'she described your surroundings, your dress, and your escort,' and here his contemptuous glance swept for a moment over Dr Raymond's person.

'She told you all this?' breathed Mary, with trembling lips.

'Angel! and it was only when I was coming here, that I was thinking of her. She is the only one I have thought about lately—and I didn't want to think about her, but I couldn't help myself, and today—oh, all day—she seemed so near!'

She seemed to have forgotten her surroundings for the moment, and sat gazing before her, in a strange, dazed way.

Tom was not slow to follow up his advantage, although not by so much as a quiver of an eyelid or the movement of a muscle did he reveal his torturing anxiety to get her away from this place and this man.

'Angel seems very ill tonight, Mary,' he said, 'and I'm afraid to think of the consequences if she doesn't see you. She has been in such constant pain also nearly all this week and her one cry, her one petition was—"Oh! if only Mary Carmichael was here!" '

Mary's face was working as she rose from her chair. Tom put her cloak around her as a matter of course, and stooping for her gloves which had fallen to the floor, he put them into her hands, for he saw her eyes were blinded with tears—and thanked God for it.

Dr Raymond sprang to his feet as he realised Mary's intention.

'Oh! but look here!' he said, 'surely you are not going off in this style? Let me come with you and wait for you. I'll—'

But Mary didn't even seem to hear him as she took Tom's arm. Indeed Charles Raymond, did he only know it, had simply ceased to exist as far as she was concerned now.

'Oh! hurry! hurry!' was all she cried. 'Oh, Tom, let us hurry!'

'I have a taxi waiting,' said Tom, and without even a backward glance they left the hotel together.

Mary Carmichael remained quite silent during the drive to Rathmines, and Tom made no effort to break her silence.

Mary Blake opened the door for them, and cried out at the sight of 'the other Mary' back once more, but Mary Carmichael would not stop a moment, and almost pushed her aside, only saying 'Angel! where is she?'

'Upstairs, in her own room,' said Mary Blake, 'go up dear—she is expecting you.'

Clare Castlemaine was with Angel when they heard the taxi stop.

'Here they are!' cried Angel, trembling with eagerness, and clasping tightly the rosary beads, which she had never laid aside since Tom had gone on his mission.

'They?' echoed Clare, doubtingly. 'How sure you seem to be, Angel—I wouldn't build too much on seeing Mary Carmichael if I were you.'

'Oh! but I am going to see her! I know!' said the other, and as if in confirmation of her words, a quick light footstep was heard running up the stairs, and the next moment the door opened and Mary Carmichael stood within the room.

Angel raised herself and opened wide her arms.

'Oh! Mary! Mary!' she cried, 'at last! Oh, you have come back to us at last!'

Mary Carmichael, kneeling beside the bed, took the frail little form into her arms—and kissed away her tears—tears of joy as they were.

'Yes, Angel, I have come back,' she said, adding brokenly, humbly, 'back to you—and back to my reason, thank God!'

'Thank God!' echoed Angel happily, as she made the sign of the cross. And Clare Castlemaine had food for serious thought as she went over these things in the solitude of her own room later that night while the little clock on the mantelpiece ticked away the minutes and the hours, and the face of our Mother of Perpetual Succour seemed to grow more pitiful and compassionate as she gazed down on that silent figure which was slowly, slowly feeling her way—slowly and painfully groping towards the Light Eternal.

CHAPTER XIII

'DEAR, COULD I ONLY TELL THEE!'

There is a country lane a little way beyond Rathfarnham and at the top of the lane—just before it branches off on the right to another road—stands an old white house. A gate and garden lead up to the jasmine covered porch. And such a garden! Dusty cyclists taking a spin into the country on hot summer afternoons, dismount and gaze at the wild riot of colour and scent within; tired city mothers and fathers who have come out by tram and then started for their Sunday walk, have hard work to keep their numerous progeny from trying to push open the gate and explore the glories within. Did Miss Arabella Blake chance to be in the garden at such a moment, the hot grimy little hands would be quickly filled with sweet blossoms, for Miss Arabella had the entire charge and control of this really wonderful old garden, and she was good nature itself, and always ready to give of its abundance to others. On the left of the porch was the dining-room window, the drawing-room on the right, and overhead the bedrooms. At the back of the house stretched the paddock and fields and poultry run; to the left the orchard and vegetable garden. Miss Anastasia Blake had care of the orchard and poultry, and Miss Jane the eldest of the three sisters was housekeeper and also looked after the accounts, for the Misses Blake did a good business by the sale of their milk and eggs.

They were Mr Blake's other sisters, and the house and land belonged to their mother, who had left it by will to her 'girls'—as they were then. They were all older than their brother and very old fashioned in their views—mid-Victorian one might say—and looked upon the present generation with a sort of surprised horror. Mary got on well with them, as was to be expected, also Tom, but Norah was too flighty, and Bride's social work was intensely disliked by them. That a young gentlewoman should have anything to do with such things! They simply could not understand it.

But with all their prejudices and rather narrow-minded views they were warm-hearted and sincere, and really loved all their brother's family. When any of the Blakes were run down or seedy, or merely out of sorts physically or mentally, a few days at Daisyfield, where they got rest of both body and mind, helped them to pull round again, and to face the battle of life once more.

And it was to this quiet refuge that Mary Carmichael had come to spend the remaining ten days of her leave. Angel accompanied her, for the sick girl had been so delighted to have her friend back again, that she seemed to have gained a new lease of life and strength, and appeared stronger than she had been for some time.

It was not, of course, Mary's first visit to Daisyfield. She was a prime favourite with 'The Aunts'—by which title the Blakes always spoke of them—and a hint from Tom about her trouble was enough to enlist all their sympathy and to cause them to welcome Mary with even more than their customary warmth.

It was a lovely May evening when she arrived, and even as she stooped under the little gate and entered the dear old garden, a feeling of peace fell upon her. As far as flowers went the garden was not yet in its full glory—although radiant enough—but away to the left was the orchard—one mass of exquisite blossom.

The three Aunts stood in the old fashioned porch to welcome her, and as she felt their gentle kisses, and heard their low-toned voices—for the Misses Blake never spoke loudly—giving her a welcome which she knew to be so sincere, the tears started unbidden to her eyes. Angel, in her basket chair—a gift from Clare—being drawn up the garden path by Tom, who was pretending to be quite exhausted by the exertion—created a welcome diversion for Mary, and by the time she was upstairs taking off her hat in the prettily draped chintz bedroom, she felt better in every way.

A real country tea was set out in the long dining-room, a good 'sit down' meal with plenty of hot cakes and home-made jam and cream, and Mary to her surprise found herself eating more than she had done for many days now. Tom and Angel—watching her with loving eyes, Angel's openly adoring, and Tom's love hidden beneath his whimsical badinage—were delighted to see the little touch of colour in her cheeks, the little look of interest in her sad eyes.

But the Aunts, who only knew a little about the recent events and had not realised how deeply she had suffered, were secretly shocked at her changed appearance, and after tea, when Mary was comfortably seated in an armchair beside Angel's couch in the sweet old drawing-room, Miss Arabella, under the pretext of showing him some special flower, wheedled Tom out into the garden and there put him through his catechism. He told her as much as he knew—which, after all, was mere outline—and her indignation knew no bounds.

'A heartless villain!' she said more bitterly than Tom ever remembered hearing her speak before, 'an ungentlemanly cur! Can you do nothing in the matter, Tom? In my young days such an insult to a young gentlewoman would not have gone unavenged.'

Tom smiled half sadly.

'*Autres temps, autres mœurs*, dear Aunt,' he said; 'If I were her brother or any relative I might take some action—but even then I don't think that Mary would let me. She cannot bear to allude to the affair at all—has never spoken of it as far as we know to anyone. And I—I have no right to approach her on the subject.'

Miss Arabella's soft, blue veined old hand was slipped into Tom's strong one, as she said softly, 'But you would like to have that right, dear boy—is it not so?'

And although her nephew did not reply in words she read her answer in the honest grey eyes looking down into hers. The following days passed peacefully, if not happily, for Mary Carmichael. Some of the Blakes came out from town every day, and Mary felt a real thrill of pleasure when Miss Jane asked Clare Castlemaine to come and stay at Daisyfield for the remainder of Mary's holiday. That holiday was getting very short now, another few days and she would be many, many miles away from her beloved Dublin.

Nurse Seeley and Daisy Ray had done all her packing for her at St Columba's, and sent on her trunks, so that she had nothing in that line to worry her. Indeed all her friends were kindness itself to her, and, benumbed with misery as she still was to a certain extent, she could not help feeling their goodness.

Something of this she mentioned to Clare one evening as they sat together after tea, under the old apple tree in the orchard.

'And I will miss you, Clare,' she said rather sadly, 'Some way we seem to have become great friends—don't we?'

'I'm glad you think so, Mary,' replied the other, 'for now I won't feel so awkward at something I want to say to you—a request I want to make.'

'A request from me!' echoed Mary in surprise. 'Why Clare, dear, anything that I can do——'

'Wait a minute!' said the other, laughing. 'Wait until you hear what I'm going to suggest! Mary, would you—would you mind very much if I came down to Co. Clare with you!'

'*Mind!*' cried Mary, 'Why you know that I should be simply delighted! But, my dear Clare, you don't know the country parts of Ireland—you don't realise——'

'That's just it,' interposed the other. 'I want to know it and to know the people. I've seen city life in Ireland and now I want to go to the country and see the life the people live there. I want to really understand their lives and ideals if I can—to feel at home with them.'

'Well, Clare, I needn't tell you how glad and thankful I will be to have you, if only for a while, for I'm afraid that you won't stay there long—the loneliness will seem dreadful to you. And then I—I, well you know that I am not—quite well these days and not myself, and I'm afraid I'll be but poor company, and scare you away before long.'

'Only try me!' said Clare.

And so the matter was settled.

Tom cycled out that evening and found Mary walking alone in the lane. She greeted him more cheerfully than usual as he dismounted and came up to her.

'Isn't it a lovely evening?' she said; 'let us take a little stroll before we go in.'

Only too gladly he complied, wheeling his bicycle and glancing now and then at the beloved face beside him.

'I wanted to speak to you, Tom,' she said after a few moments' silence. 'There is no one else who understands me as well as you do—no one else to whom I could speak as I am going to speak to you.'

'My dear,' he said softly—brokenly.

But she went on as though she had not heard him.

'Tom, you know—you have guessed that God has sent me a terrible cross to bear—a cross that seemed to me at first unbearable, and that even now is—very heavy. I—I was nearly falling under it altogether, and only for Angel—dear, dear little Angel! I think I would have been lost, but her angelic spirit in some wonderful way reached to me when I was at the very gates of Hell and brought me back in spite of myself.'

She paused, trembling, and Tom, leaning his bicycle against the hedge, took both her hands in his and held them firmly.

She looked up at him pitifully.

'Tom,' she whispered, so low that he had to stoop to hear her, 'I—I have wandered very far from God these past days, and I want to—to go to Confession.'

He nodded quietly, while his grey eyes lit up and his honest heart leapt with joy within him.

'Tom!' lower still, and with trembling voice, 'I'm afraid! I don't know *why*—I think it is because I'm so broken up and nervous—but Confession seems to me now to be an ordeal that I can never get through. But oh! I want to go. Tomorrow will be Saturday, and on Wednesday you know I leave Dublin.'

Just as if he had not the very days counted!

'You will get Confession tomorrow, dear,' he said, gently, tenderly as one speaks to a frightened child, and still holding her hands in his.

'That is what I want,' she said, 'and, Tom, I want you—Oh! I want you to come to the church with me and wait for me—will you? It will not be so hard then.'

Tom Blake's self-command was almost gone.

'Oh! my dear!—my dear!' was all he could say.

'You *will* then?' she said. 'Oh, Tom, thank you so much—so much!'

'For God's sake don't thank me, Mary!' he said then, crushing the hands he held almost fiercely to his breast; 'don't thank me! don't you *know*—don't you realise—'

He stopped abruptly, for she was looking at him in puzzled surprise, and immediately Tom pulled himself together again. He was her friend—she had so far honoured him—and now was he going to spoil it all by——

'Then tomorrow I will call for you,' he said in his pleasant every-day tones, and releasing her hands gently he turned to his bicycle again, 'and now if we don't make tracks for home the aunts will be thinking we are lost!'

When they came in sight of the house they saw Shamus Blake leaning over the garden gate. He waved his hat as they came near and opening the gate went down the road to meet them.

'Anthony O'Farrell is here,' he said—Shamus, of course, always gave Anthony the Irish prefix—'he only heard you were going south today,' he added to Mary, 'and as he knows that part very well he wanted to have a talk with you.'

Mary would rather not have seen Anthony Farrell again—for they had not met since Easter, and she knew that he, in common with the rest of her world, had expected that she would shortly be settled in Dublin, and not be leaving for the country like this.

But she smiled faintly in assent and slipped her hand into that of Shamus, for like all those who knew him she was intensely fond of the brilliant enthusiastic Irish boy.

'Well—Shamus! how goes the world with you?' she asked, 'and how are all the Irish Irelanders these times?'

'Oh! we are all right!' he answered gaily; 'all working hard; working and praying for the dear old land! You know, Mary,' he went on more seriously, 'things may look dark for Ireland now—for of course you know what *we* think of this Home Rule myth. But mind you, the day is coming—and sooner perhaps than you think—when a torch will be lighted, and when it is lighted it will run like wild fire throughout the length and breadth of the land, and in every county will a spark fall—sparks that will burst into flame and purge the bad from the good, and purify this beloved land of ours!'

Mary smiled—but tenderly.

'Ah! well, Shamus dear,' she said, 'don't be doing anything rash. We wouldn't like to think of you getting into any sort of trouble.'

'*Trouble!*' echoed the boy. 'Why Mary, do you think I would mind any trouble—any hardship—do you think I would grudge the last drop of blood in my body if it was for Ireland! Oh, Mary, I often and often think what an honour—what a joy unspeakable it would be for me, if I *could* only say when Death called me—"This is for Ireland!"'

Mary shivered suddenly—why, she did not know then, but two years later she knew and understood.

Entering the quaint drawing-room they found only Angel and the aunts. Clare Castlemaine and Anthony Farrell were out in the orchard and there we will follow them and find them seated under the old apple tree.

Clare had been telling him that she had arranged to accompany Mary Carmichael to the country, and Anthony had listened in a strangely silent and preoccupied mood.

'You know that part of Ireland—don't you?' she was saying. 'What are the people like?—and the country—is it pretty?'

'The people?' echoed her companion rousing himself with an effort. 'Oh *well*, you will have to go there to understand them—that is, if you ever *will* understand them, for it's a difficult job for a stranger. As for the country some of it is extremely wild, and other parts really beautiful but none of it is merely pretty.'

'Tell me,' he continued, 'what made you get this notion into your head? For you know I don't believe that you will ever stick it—the loneliness, for anyone not used to it, is dreadful.'

'Exactly what Mary said when I told her I wanted to go with her,' said Clare, 'but it will be such a new experience for me—so interesting that I don't believe I will be dull at all. And then—well! I have a special reason for going with Mary Carmichael just now.'

Anthony gave her a keen glance, as he said quietly—'You want to watch her spiritual condition—so to speak? To see if the Catholic Faith as exemplified by Mary Carmichael is worthy of your consideration or not?'

Clare's hands shook a little as she idly pulled a bit of laburnum to pieces.

'Well—yes,' she said at last, 'I suppose that is my reason more or less.'

There was silence for a few minutes, and then Anthony spoke again very softly.

'Are you still in doubt, Clare? Can you not see even a glimmer of the Light of Faith yet?'

'A glimmer—yes,' she answered, brokenly, 'but the bright light that will scatter the darkness from round my path—*that* has not come yet!'

'But—with God's help—it *will*,' replied the man, reverently.

'I have a strange idea,' went on the girl, 'that in some way I am to find that which I am seeking during my time in the country. I was told when I came to Ireland that I would there find my Irish heritage. In Dublin I have just seen visions of it—but I think that perhaps amidst the cabins by the bogs and hillsides I will find the treasure.'

He smiled at her tenderly, and laid his hand on hers—'Clare,' he said, 'you *know* what I want to say. Will I speak now, or later when you have found that for which you are seeking?'

She smiled at him through her sudden tears.

'Wait!' she whispered, 'for a little while! Wait until I have found my Irish heritage.'

CHAPTER XIV

'DAWN'

It was a lovely day in the last week of Our Lady's beautiful month, when Mary Carmichael and Clare Castlemaine left the city for the green fields and pastures of Co. Clare.

Mary gazed with indifferent and unseeing eyes at the country through which they were passing. She had felt the parting from the Blakes, and especially had she suffered in saying good-bye to Angel, who had clung to her almost frantically, but even that parting affected her very little in comparison with what it would have done under different circumstances. The terrible shock and grief through which she had just passed seemed to have used up nearly all the feeling which she possessed, and to have left her incapable of either grief or pain to any great extent, and she was absolutely indifferent as to where she was going, or what her future was to be.

Clare, on the contrary, looked with intense interest at everything that was to be seen from her carriage window. She was feeling happier than she had felt for many a day—a strange feeling of rest and peace was upon her, and she was looking forward to her new life in the country with the joyful anticipation of a school-girl. The scenery had gradually been changing in its aspect as they went further south, and now the low stone walls which divide the fields and which are such a land-mark in Co. Clare appeared. Then stretches of bogland, with the pretty little bog flower waving in the breeze; here and there was seen a cabin with bare-legged youngsters waving at the train as it passed, and perhaps their mother—her scarlet petticoat making a bright spot of colour against the brown bog—would pause for a moment in her work to gaze also at the rushing monster.

'Oh, Mary!' cried Clare, 'do look at those goats and the dear little kids. And the boy with them—oh, it's just like an academy picture I saw last year.'

They were nearing Limerick, where they had to change, and to wait for over an hour for the local train which was to take them—at its leisure—to the end of their journey.

Mary Carmichael had once been in Limerick for a few weeks visiting a school friend. It was now some years ago and her friend was no longer there but she remembered the town pretty well, and volunteered to show Clare around a bit, after they had had some tea.

So she piloted her about the sleepy, quaint, old city, and as they stood before the Treaty Stone, Clare listened with surprise to the story of the Treaty—'Broken ere the ink wherewith 'twas writ could dry.'

'But, Mary,' she said, 'I don't remember ever learning that in my history lessons?'

'No, I don't suppose you did,' said Mary drily; 'it's very likely that you didn't hear much about the penal days either, or Cromwell's marches through the land, or how the people were treated in '98, or even how the dastardly Act of Union was really passed?'

'You are right,' said Clare, half inclined to smile at Mary's earnestness, 'but those are all old tales now—don't let us talk about them! Remember I have English blood in my veins, and between us these things are best forgotten!'

To her surprise the other turned upon her almost fiercely. 'For *you*—yes!' she said, 'but they will never be forgotten by us.'

'But, Mary,' returned Clare, totally unable to understand her friend's bitterness, 'all this is over and past, and surely you know that however badly England may have treated Ireland in the past, it was only because it was the way of the world then to be cruel, and to take heavy revenges. Why, supposing—I know, of course, it's nonsense to even think of such a thing!—but just suppose for the sake of argument that there was to be another Irish rebellion in these days, don't you know very well that England would show no cruelty or avenge herself in any way on the people. Why surely you know that if such a thing happened now the English people would act towards Ireland with justice and mercy.'

To her somewhat indignant surprise Mary Carmichael laughed. And it was a *real* laugh—such as she had not heard from her lately.

'Oh, Clare! you innocent baby,' she said; 'is that all you know about your father's country? To believe that the English would act towards Ireland with justice and mercy! Oh! it's too much!' and she laughed again.

Clare felt offended and hurt.

'Well! *how* would they act then?' she asked stiffly.

'They would doubtless act as they have always acted since they first set foot on our shores over seven hundred years ago,' answered the other, her laughter gone and her face suddenly pale with anger; 'they would act with treachery and deceit, with brutality and cruelty, and would justify it all on the stupid plea of doing good to Ireland.'

'Well, really, if that's what you think about England,' began Clare—but Mary, with one of those swift changes of manner which was one of her greatest charms, slipped her arm within Clare's and laughed away her resentment.

'Come! we mustn't quarrel!' she said, 'and after all you are *barely* half English! Oh! how thankful you should be for that! Come and see the Redemptorist Church—if that won't convert you nothing will!'

And so together they wended their way to Mount St Alphonsus—surely one of the most beautiful churches in this land where Faith has built so many lovely dwelling places for the 'Prisoner of Love'. On Clare it had a most extraordinary effect—it impressed her as no other of the Catholic churches which she had visited had ever done. A sense of peace and rest fell upon her, and as she knelt with Mary before the Shrine of Our Lady of Perpetual Succour, she found herself almost involuntarily breathing her first prayer. It was more a thought—a wish—than a prayer.

'Oh! Mother!' she said—'if you are indeed our Mother—and if you have any power in Heaven—show it to me now—and help me!' Such as it was, surely it went straight to our dear Mother's heart. Mary was praying too—but very differently. Hers was the prayer of the Catholic who *knew* and *believed*, but who had wandered from the straight path which was set before her feet. And her prayer over and over again was only the old familiar 'Oh! Mother of Perpetual Succour, pray for me; pray for *me*! Oh, Mary conceived without sin, pray for me—a sinner!'

• • •

Later that same evening the two friends sat at supper in a little four-roomed ivy-covered cottage. There was a wood opposite and a field with great grey boulders scattered over it, behind them. Not a sound was to be heard but the birds singing their evensong in the trees and the persistent coo-coo of innumerable wood pigeons. It seemed very strange and lonely that first evening to those two—so accustomed all their lives to the stir and bustle of city life. But although Clare was lonely she was not unhappy—rather the opposite indeed—for she felt the most intense interest in all her surroundings. The drive of four miles from the station on the shaky old sidecar, the handsome, dark-eyed driver, who had such a twinkle in his eye, and seemed to find life such a good joke—the fat, little servant girl who had shaken hands so cordially with them on their arrival! All had amused and interested Clare—all were picturesque and new to her. But with Mary it was otherwise. She had never liked the country—its beauty had never appealed to her in any shape or form, and to her the people were stupid and uninteresting—the scenery lonely and weird. That first night she hardly slept at all, and often looked enviously at Clare, sleeping so peacefully in the other bed—her tranquil breathing barely heard even in the stillness of the night. Poor Mary turned her face to the wall and great tears forced their way from her tired eyes as she thought again and again, 'Oh! how can I bear it! *How* can I bear it!'

The days passed, and both became more used to their new life. Mary gradually found her work more and more absorbing, and it took up so much of her time that she had but little left for repining, or 'grousing' as she herself would have said in the old days.

Clare should have been the lonelier of the two for she had not much to do except to train the little maid-servant and to see that the house was kept neat and clean, and the meals made as tasty and appetising as possible for Mary, who sometimes would come in after cycling many miles in wind and wet—for it seemed to be always wet in Co. Clare, summer and winter—too tired almost to eat at all. But Clare did not feel the loneliness, she busied herself in a hundred ways and sewed and read, and undertook nearly all their correspondence, for somehow Mary did not care to write to any of her friends—with the exception of Angel who got her regular weekly letter no matter how pressed for time Mary might be. And Clare, too, was not forgetful of the treasure for which she was searching. Into the cabin and homes around her she went, welcomed everywhere with the natural politeness of a people who numbered princes and kings for their ancestors. In nearly every house was the old grandmother telling her beads by the fireside, and many a story Clare heard from them of 'the bad times' and many a lesson in resignation and patience she learnt by their armchairs. 'Himself' was dead, the sons and daughters perhaps in 'Amerikay', all save this one daughter or son under whose roof the old woman was spending the evening of her days. Ah! yes, she was lonely sometimes, but sure welcome be the Will of God!

'Welcome be the Will of God!' How often and how often Clare heard that sentence amongst the poor peasantry around her. And again 'God is good!' Yes, the winter had been hard sure enough, and the cows had died on them, and the young calf too, and herself was ailing this long time, and the children young and troublesome, but sure God is good, and maybe she would soon be well again. And so on—always the same expressions of love and trust in God's mercy, and the same perfect faith that never doubted or wavered for a moment, that never—no matter how heavy the cross, how staggering the blow—wavered in allegiance, or even questioned His right to do as He pleased with His Own.

'Oh! what faith! What faith!' Clare would say, as she walked home from some house of sorrow or trouble. 'Oh! what would I not give to be able to say with these poor people—"Welcome be the Will of God!"'

Another thing that struck Clare very forcibly was the utter contrast spiritually, mentally and morally between the Irish peasant and the corresponding class of English labourer. She remembered a short time she had spent on a farm in England, and had very vivid recollections of some of the farm hands whom she had met. Stupid, heavy and dull, with apparently no ideals or aims, no aspirations beyond meat and beer. Sunday meant a day in bed till dinner time, and then a heavy dinner, and more sleeping, to be followed by more drink. Clare, at that time had regarded them as very little above the farm animals around them, and indeed if truth were told she infinitely preferred the animals.

She contrasted these now with the clean souled, spiritual people of her present home. She thought of the many miles they walked winter and summer to the little village chapel for early Mass, of the family Rosary at night, of the intellectual, bright eyed young men who would answer all her remarks or questions, so civilly, and yet so intelligently, with often a spark of humour showing, too. And she thought of the young girls—those modest, low toned Catholic girls of Ireland, with the lovely grey eyes and the soft dusky hair—and then she remembered suddenly some of the Cockney 'Arriets, flaunting, loudvoiced, loudly dressed beings, disgracing the sacred name of woman. 'Shamus is right,' she murmured with a sigh, 'they *are* a different people—a different race.'

And then she turned her thought to Mary Carmichael, and watched how the Catholic Faith slowly but surely was laying a healing hand on her wounded heart. She noticed Mary at her prayers, at her daily work—so painstaking, so conscientious, so kind—above all at Mass and Holy Communion. And she saw daily the hardness die out of her face and eyes, and a gentler look take its place, a more tender tone in her voice. And thus she knew that Mary Carmichael also was saying in her own way, 'Welcome be the Will of God.'

And so the summer months of June and July passed quietly by, and then came August and the War—and Clare was immediately all excitement and full of patriotic fervour, and talked about 'the Empire' and how 'We'—in capital letters of course!—would be in Berlin by Christmas. And Mary Carmichael was silent, but she smiled in a queer fashion now and then at Clare's remarks.

After another few months Mary even felt a little sorry for her friend when day after day the news from the British standpoint became worse and worse, and alas! the marching on Berlin became but a dream—and the shadow of a dream!

'How *can* you take things so easily, Mary?' said Clare, almost angrily one evening, throwing aside the newspaper in which she had been engrossed. They did not get the newspaper until mid-day and Clare was always in a state of anxiety until she had mastered its contents.

'Why, what do you want me to do?' asked Mary.

'Well! I know what I should do if I were a trained nurse,' replied Clare, 'I should volunteer for the front without a moment's delay.'

'Very likely,' said Mary, quietly, 'but you see, Clare, I am not you, and you are not me! I have no English blood in my veins—some Scotch is mixed with the Irish certainly, but that,' with a little laugh—'is a very decent mixture!'

But Clare wouldn't smile.

'I don't know how you can joke about serious things; Mary,' she said, rather stiffly, 'and at a time like this when the life of every one of our gallant soldiers is so valuable, and when the very Empire itself is at stake——'

'Oh! spare me!—*please!*' implored Mary, half vexed, half laughing, 'if there are three words at the present moment of which I am heartily sick and tired—those three words are—the British Empire!'

Clare said no more, but she felt both hurt and offended. It was quite impossible for her to understand Mary's feelings at the time.

Entirely ignorant of even the main facts relating to English rule in Ireland—with the exception of a few outlines which she had picked up from her cousin Shamus and Anthony Farrell, and which she had honestly regarded as being certainly exaggerated—she could not view the war from an Irish standpoint, and although Mary never expressed any pro-German sympathies, or even made a single anti-British remark, still Clare felt—her instinct told her—that Mary's feelings were more anti-British than merely neutral.

But Mary was really more or less indifferent to the trend of events.

The war had come at a time when she was only beginning to regain her normal state once more and to take a healthy interest in her work and surroundings. And so important to ourselves is that strange ego of ours that it takes precedence in our eyes before all the principalities and kingdoms of the world. So Mary, half benumbed yet, her feelings still dulled, really took but little interest in the great war, and like most people, as the weeks went on into months, and the months became a year, she got so used to it that she almost ceased to think of it.

Not so Clare—her interest and anxiety only became greater as time went on, and especially did she dilate on the terrible atrocities of the 'Huns'.

Mary generally let her run on without contradiction, but one evening when she was holding forth more than usual about the poor Belgian babies left to go through life without hands, etc., she saw Mary smiling broadly, and gazed at her in disgust and horror.

'Mary!' she cried, 'you are laughing!—at such atrocities!'

Mary continued to smile, as she replied, 'I am smiling at you Clare—not at the English version of German horrors. You are not a trained nurse, I know, but surely even *you* know that when a hand or an arm is severed from the body, and no surgical treatment applied, that the person will bleed to death in a very short time.'

Clare said nothing, but sat quite silent, looking at Mary in half stupid surprise—it was evident that she had not thought of this fact before.

So time went on, and another spring and summer passed by and Christmas 1915 arrived. That Christmas they spent in the old 'City of the Broken Treaty,' and from a spiritual point of view it was a very memorable one for both.

They attended first Mass in the darkness of Christmas morning at the Redemptorist Church, and when Clare rose from her knees she knew that for her all doubts and strivings were over—and what that doubting time had been only God and herself could tell. But all was over now—her path showed clear before her and Clare was not one to turn her back on the light when it had been given to her—she would never take her hand from the plough once her work was shown to her. She had hesitated for long—too long, she thought now—but God in His wonderful mercy had flashed His light upon her in the darkness of this Christmas dawn—and like a child running to its mother—she turned at last straight to the arms of her Mother the Church.

She told Mary of her resolution as they sat together that evening, and Mary's eyes filled with sudden tears.

'Oh! Clare, dear,' she said, 'I am *so* glad!—so thankful!' Her own time of 'storm and stress', followed by the 'peace which passeth understanding', came back to Mary as she spoke, and she broke off with a little sob—but, as Clare was quick to see, there was no bitterness or sorrow in her tears.

'You seemed so happy too this morning, Mary,' she said. 'I could not help noticing your face as you returned from the Altar, and you looked *happy* as well as peaceful. And you know, Mary, it is not often lately that you have looked really happy.'

'I know dear,' said the other, 'I have not felt either very happy or very unhappy, or very *anything* for a long time! I haven't been feeling at all. But this morning—Oh! Clare, the dear little Infant Jesus, when He came to my heart brought me some real joy and happiness for my Christmas gift; and I so unworthy—oh, so unworthy!'

'Unworthy! *You!*' interposed Clare, 'Oh, Mary, don't! If you only knew what your example, your silent endurance, your cheerful patience——'

'Oh, stop! stop!' cried the other, clapping her hands over her ears, half laughing and half crying—'don't make me vain for goodness' sake!'

Then putting her arms round Clare she said softly, 'There is someone else, too, who will be glad of your news. Poor Anthony! Don't you think he has been very patient Clare?'

'Yes—I think so!' said Clare, with a tender little smile. 'But Mary, he always knew that I would some day come into my Irish Heritage.'

CHAPTER XV

THE CALL OF DARK ROSALEEN

Oh! the Erne shall run red
With redundance of blood,
The earth shall rock beneath our tread,
And flames wrap hill and wood;
And gun peal and slogan cry
Wake many a glen serene,
Ere you shall fade, ere you shall die,
My dark Rosaleen!
My own Rosaleen!
The judgment hour must first be nigh,
Ere you can fade, ere you can die,
My dark Rosaleen!

The first few months of 1916 passed quietly but happily for our two friends. Clare was busy preparing for her Reception into the Catholic Church, in March, going twice weekly into Limerick for instruction, and reading and praying earnestly. As for Mary Carmichael she was certainly happier and more interested than she had been since her great trouble; she seemed to be living over again those past days when she, like Clare, stood 'on the Threshold,' looking half fearfully, half longingly at the wondrous 'Mystery of Faith' within the Sanctuary. She was of untold help and comfort to Clare, helping her over many a difficulty, and explaining much that troubled her. No one can understand a convert's point of view—their difficulties and trials, their doubts and fears, so well as another convert. The same hard road, walked often with tired and bleeding feet, has to be gone over, the same trials—a smile here, a sneer there—have to be borne. Each individual case naturally has his or her own special cross at this time, but they have so much in common, no matter how differently they may be situated, that there is always a strong bond between them.

One thing, which is the source of great pain to many converts, was spared to Clare Castlemaine. She had no other religious beliefs to give up—for her there was no wrenching away from the old faiths, the old ideals. Catholics who are born in the Faith cannot realise that a would-be convert can possibly have much to give up from a spiritual point of view; to their mind one has nothing to lose and all to gain on entering the Catholic Church. They are right of course. But human nature is human nature, and one clings almost insensibly to the hymns one sang as a child to 'Grannie' on Sunday afternoons, and to the prayers—imperfect though they be—which were learned at our mother's knee. Clare had no such regrets, and neither had she the greater bitterness of seeing her nearest and dearest turn away from her—to find herself cut off from the friends of her girlhood, and to be cast more or less adrift except for her new friends on earth and 'the millions of new friends in Heaven,'—as a nun once said to a recent convert who had been left very desolate by her own people.

She was baptised on the 15th of March and made her First Communion on St Patrick's Day. Mary had obtained a week's holiday, and they went to Limerick together.

Clare was almost frightened at the thrill of perfect happiness which she experienced as she knelt at the Altar rails. She had been very nervous—although not at all of a nervous type—and felt herself actually shaking as she heard, as though in a dream, the voice of the priest coming nearer and nearer—

'Corpus Domini nostri Jesu Christi——'

The next moment He had come to her. He had waited long, but as though to show His forgiveness and love, He now poured forth into her heart that 'perfect peace that passeth understanding.'

Yet of the two girls, Mary was the more moved. She had none of Clare's English temperament, which can often hide its deepest feelings under a calm—almost cold—exterior, and the tears were running down her face as she groped her way back to her seat. Never had the two loved each other more or felt more in sympathy with each other than on this March morning when they gave each other the 'kiss of peace' in the little sitting-room of their lodgings after their return from Mass.

Anthony Farrell came down from Dublin for a day shortly afterwards, and Clare's happiness was complete. It was arranged that they were to be married after the summer.

'So I must look out for another companion,' said Mary, trying to smile bravely, although her eyes betrayed her pain.

It was the one blot on Clare's happiness. She knew that Mary would not return to Dublin, and it went to her heart to leave her in loneliness.

'It's nearly two years now since it happened,' she said to Anthony, when they were alone together, 'and I do believe that it is as fresh as ever in her mind—and as painful.'

'What a pity she should waste her thoughts over such a cad as Delaney,' said Farrell regretfully; 'if only she would think of poor Tom Blake! Do you think he has a chance at all, Clare, or ever will?'

'Oh! I'm afraid not! I'm afraid not!' replied the girl; 'she doesn't even realise that he cares for her!'

'Ah, well,' said Anthony, with a half smile, 'Father Time is a wonderful old fellow—a better healer than all the physicians in the world. Who knows what the future has in store for her?'

Before going, he spoke a few words to Mary herself, but on a different subject—a subject that he had not mentioned at all to Clare. His words caused Mary to turn very white, and look at him with dilated eyes.

'But not *yet*, Tony,' she breathed; 'not *soon*?'

'Sooner than you think perhaps,' he said briefly, and turned away as Clare entered.

Easter Sunday and Monday passed peacefully and quietly in the little Co. Clare village, the inhabitants of which little dreamt of the tragedy already begun in Dublin city.

The two girls were in the habit of repeating the Rosary together at night, and at its close on Easter Monday, Mary astonished Clare by suddenly bursting into tears—violent heart-breaking sobs that shook her from head to foot.

'Mary! Mary! my dear! What is it?' cried Clare.

But only sobs answered her.

'Mary!' she cried again, now really alarmed—this was so unlike Mary—'What is the matter? please tell me!'

'Oh! Clare! Clare,' sobbed the other, '*I don't know*! I don't know what it is; but Oh! I wish I was back in Dublin—I'm wanted there!'

'Wanted in Dublin?' repeated the other, in puzzled tones; 'but, Mary, if the Blakes or anyone else wanted you they would surely send for you.'

Mary was trying to regain command of herself, and partly succeeded. 'I don't really know what *is* wrong with me, Clare,' she said, trying pitifully to smile; 'nerves, I suppose!—rather a new state for me!'

'Yes; but, Mary, what did you mean about Dublin?—and being wanted there?'

Mary rose rather unsteadily from her knees, and looked at Clare with a strangely worried look.

'I can hardly explain,' she said, in a troubled voice; 'a most overwhelming longing came over me to go back to Dublin at once, and I seemed to feel as if my native city was calling aloud to me!—calling me to return. Clare, I *know*—I am sure something has happened there!'

'Something has happened in Dublin?' repeated Clare, half amused. 'What nonsense, Mary, you must be over-tired, you have had such a hard time lately. Let us get to bed early, and you will feel better in the morning.'

Next day Mary was in the village about post time—they had one delivery early in the morning, but had to call for their mid-day letters—and she entered the little Post Office to inquire for letters and to get her newspaper.

She was surprised to observe quite a crowd round the door, and excited comments and remarks were being freely exchanged.

'Good day, Miss Phelan,' Mary said, going up to the counter, 'any letters for me?'

'Oh! there are no letters at all, Nurse!' replied the little woman who kept the Post Office and fancy shop combined; 'the Sinn Féiners have broken out in Dublin, and there are no mails or papers. I only got a few words over the wire from Limerick, and they are cut off from Dublin already, and we can get no news from anywhere!'

Mary Carmichael reeled against the counter.

'Are you *sure*? Oh! are you sure it's true?' she asked, putting out her shaking hands to steady herself.

'Oh, it's true, Miss—sure enough!' replied the woman. 'Come into the room beyond, and I'll get you a glass of water. Sure I forget ye were from the city, Miss, and will have friends up there!'

How she got home eventually, Mary never remembered—it was like a dream, or rather a terrible nightmare like the days and nights that followed—a nightmare of horror and cruelty and murder—an orgy of bloodshed from which there seemed to be no awakening.

During the first few days—against her better judgement—Mary had tried to hope for the best, especially as the most inspiring rumours of all kinds reached the village in some extraordinary way.

An Irish Republic was firmly established—English rule in Ireland was over—finished for ever—and so on. But with the first newspaper that drifted in all her hopes and dreams vanished like smoke. She would never forget that evening when Clare came running to the cottage with the paper clenched in her hand. Mary almost tore it from her grasp, but with one agonised glance at the headlines it fell to the floor, and Mary was lying beside it in a perfect agony of sorrow and desolation. Clare had no comfort to give—no words to say. She read the paper in silence, trying to realise what it meant for her mother's country, for her new friends—for her cousins in Dublin—and, above all—for love is ever selfish though perhaps unconsciously so—for Anthony Farrell. Was he in the Rising, she wondered? That his sympathies were with them she knew, but whether he would take an active part or not was another matter.

'Mary,' she said, putting out a trembling hand to the sobbing girl, 'what about the Blakes?—and Tony?'

'Oh, if I only knew!' sobbed the other. 'Mother of God! if I only knew! Oh, Shamus! Shamus!'

Clare started. In her fear for her lover she had forgotten this cousin of hers.

'Oh! yes—Shamus!' she exclaimed, 'he is sure to be in it—isn't he?'

'Sure!' replied Mary briefly.

Then she raised herself and staggered to a chair.

'Oh! Clare!' she said, 'if I was only there! if I was only there! I would give anything in the world to be with them now!'

The next day's papers came, and the next, and still the dreadful massacres went on. Then came news of the North King Street shootings, of the Portobello murders, and many other revelations of what English martial law means for Ireland.

Truth to tell Clare was aghast. Never for one moment had she honestly believed that her father's countrymen would have acted in this matter with such an utter absence of the merest dictates of humanity—not to speak of justice or mercy. And for the first time in her life she was ashamed of her English origin. And yet all this time Mary Carmichael never said one word of the 'I told you so' type. Clare wondered had she forgotten their conversation in Limerick on the day when they had journeyed from Dublin together, and she had been so offended when Mary laughed at the idea of English justice for Ireland.

As for Mary herself she was suffering as she had never thought she would again after her other trouble. For days she practically did without either food or sleep—and never felt the want of them. Many of the leaders had been dear friends of hers, and others had been known to her by reputation, and through the talk of Shamus. As for him, she never doubted for one moment that he had given his life for his 'darling Rosaleen'—for his dear, ill-fated land—the land that all down through the centuries has always had, and always will have, the power to bring under her banner all the best and brightest, and purest of young Irish manhood.

Mary had wired to the Blakes as soon as telegraphic communication was re-established, but she had received no reply, and Clare had wired to Tony with a similar result.

That week was one that neither of them ever wished to look back upon—but alas! it could never be forgotten—it was never to be erased from their memory.

And then one evening in the second week Clare was standing at the gate of the cottage, looking down the road, when she suddenly gave a cry that brought Mary to her side.

Anthony Farrell was approaching the cottage, but—was it really Anthony? As he reached the gate both exclaimed at his appearance, and Clare, with a quick sob, went straight to his arms.

'Oh! Tony, Tony!' she said, when she could speak, 'how you must have suffered!'

A spasm of pain crossed his haggard and drawn features as he turned to greet Mary. Her shaking lips formed the word, 'Shamus?'

Anthony did not answer in words, but, alas! it was not necessary.

'It is only what I expected, Tony,' Mary said with the quietness of despair; 'but, thank God, that you are safe. Come in now, and tell us all. We have gone through days of such misery and suspense that *any* news—even the worst—will be better for us.'

Anthony followed her into the cottage and flung himself into a chair.

'Oh, Mary, Mary! God help me,' he said. 'How am I to tell you at all?'

CHAPTER XVI

AFTERMATH

To every man upon this earth death cometh soon or late,
And how can man die better than facing fearful odds
For the ashes of his fathers, and the temples of his gods.

There was silence for a few moments in Mary's little sitting-room, and then Anthony straightened himself suddenly, and seemed to brace himself for what he had to say. Clare was seated in a low chair beside him, her hand in his, and Mary was seated opposite to him, her eyes never leaving his face.

'It is no good keeping you longer in suspense,' he said at last. 'Shamus was shot in action in the Post Office area. He was helping a wounded comrade to safety when an English bullet hit him—two indeed. One only grazed his temple the other entered the lung.'

Clare was sobbing, but Mary sat stiff and upright in her chair. Every vestige of colour had left her face, and her eyes were strained and hard, but she was quite calm.

'Did he die at once?' she asked.

'No,' replied Anthony, 'he was shot in the morning, about eleven o'clock, and did not die till ten at night. We got him——'

Clare interrupted him quickly.

'We!' she said. 'Oh, Tony, then you were in it too?'

He looked at her in surprise.

'Why, certainly,' he said; 'surely you would not have wished me to stand aside at such a time? I was not one who voted for the Rising; but when it was an accomplished fact my place was with my countrymen. I was in the GPO during all the fighting, and escaped almost by a miracle.'

'Go on about Shamus,' said Mary, and her voice sounded hard and cold.

'Well! We got him into a friend's house for safety, and a doctor and nurse saw him at once. Ah! Mary, I can never tell you how devotedly our Red Cross people worked. We had a priest also, and he received the Last Sacraments. I asked him,'—Tony's voice broke suddenly, but he struggled on, 'I asked him had he any request to make, or was there anything that I could do for him. And he asked me to bring his sister Mary to him if possible.'

'And did you?' breathed Clare.

'Yes. I can never forget that journey to Rathmines—it was bad enough going, but coming back with Mary it was an awful ordeal. But she was very brave. How we escaped I don't know—I suppose it was to be—anyhow we got safely to where poor Shamus was lying. That was about eight o'clock, and he was anxiously awaiting us, for he knew he had not much longer to live. Mary just went straight to him and knelt beside him, holding his hand, but she could not speak. He smiled at her with all his old brave spirit, although his eyes were dimmed with pain. He gave her messages for all the others, and for Norah Donovan. She was in the College of Surgeons with the Countess, and we could not reach her. Presently Shamus asked us to say the Rosary in Irish—there were about six of us with him—and we did so. A little before ten o'clock, he turned to me and said—the words coming very slowly and with difficulty—"If you get out of this all right, old fellow, tell Mary Carmichael that I have got my wish." I don't know what he meant of course, but that is his message! He seemed to slumber for a few moments, and then he opened his eyes suddenly and looked straight at the foot of the bed. No one was there—that we could see—but he—he lifted his hand to the salute and saying quite loudly and clearly—"For Ireland!" he fell back—dead!'

'Yes—he got his wish!' said Mary, letting the tears fall at last.

'And the others!' asked Clare. 'Oh! are they all right?'

Anthony did not speak at once. Then—

'Mary and Norah and Bride are with Mr Blake in Rathmines,' he said, 'and as for Pat, he was a perfect brick all through that terrible time—dressing our wounded, and doing the work of two men. He is at present "lying low," as he would say himself, because there are several of our people in hiding who need his care, and so he is still in the city, and has not returned to Rathmines yet.'

'And Tom?' It was Mary who asked the question.

Anthony rose abruptly from his seat and going to the window, stood looking our for a few moments. There was a white lilac tree outside, and the scent was wafted to him through the open casement. He could never bear the smell of lilac afterwards.

'And Tom?' repeated Mary again, and her voice sounded strange in her ears.

'Tom was shot,' and Anthony turned suddenly and put his arm round Mary as a stifled moan fell upon his ears. She could not speak, but looked at him pitifully and he went on quickly—trying to get it over—to put her out of suspense—and feeling, as we feel when we have hurt some poor dumb thing.

'Tom did not join them at first,' he said, 'he thought, like myself that the Rising was a mistake at the time, but on the third day he went to his father, and told him that he could not stay at home any longer—both Shamus and Pat were gone, and he must follow if only to see could he gain any tidings of them. His father had expected this. "No Blake ever hung back when his country called him"—he said—"your grandfather was out in '67—and I only wish to God that I was young myself again!" Even Mary did not try to dissuade him. He made his way citywards, and had not gone far when he fell in with some young fellows whom he knew. They gave him a rifle and he joined them—one of them was a special friend of Shamus. Coming to a place where the firing was pretty severe they had to stop and defend themselves against the British. They fought for over two hours and both sides were pretty well exhausted.

'Tom's attention, it seems, was suddenly caught by the sight of a wounded British soldier lying in the very centre of the roadway—a perfect target for the rifles of both sides. Without an instant's hesitation he stepped out of the ranks. "Where are you going?" said the man who fought beside him, and who happened to be his brother's friend, from whom I heard it all. "I want to drag that Tommy out of the firing line—he's badly hit, poor chap!" Tom replied.

'"You'll be a fool if you do!" said the other; "do you think that they would do as much for one of us?"'

'"I can't help it," replied Tom, "I couldn't see any unfortunate wretch suffering like that."'

'Oh! how like him!' whispered Mary, as Anthony paused for a moment.

'Well, he reached the soldier, and managed to bring him to the Irish ranks. He had just placed him in safety behind the firing line, and was returning to his place, when an English bullet was aimed straight at him, and he fell at once, shot through the heart.'

Mary did not attempt to speak, and Clare sat aghast.

'His friends got the body, and he was buried with the Flag of the Irish Republic wrapped round him.'

Mary lifted her drawn face. 'And Angel?' she breathed. 'Oh, Tony, don't tell me that she too——'

'No, dear!—no!' he reassured her quickly. 'The shock has been terrible of course for her, and for days we thought that she was going to join her brothers; but God means to spare her to us for a little while yet; and Mary—I have one bit of pleasant news for you—she is coming down to stay with you for a long visit as soon as she is able for the journey.'

'Thank God!' said Mary.

Then she rose and laid her hand on Anthony's arm.

'Thank you, Tony,' she said quietly, 'I know what it must have cost you to have to speak of these things. God bless you for coming. Now I want to be alone for a while, and I will leave you with Clare.'

There was silence for a few minutes when she left the room.

'Clare,' said Anthony then.

But there was no answer—Clare's sweet face was hidden in her hands, and her head was bent down on the arm of her chair.

He was beside her instantly.

'Dearest!' he said softly, 'don't fret—sure, it is the Will of God!'

'I'm not fretting—at least not for them,' was the stifled answer.

'Then for what?' he asked.

Her face was still hidden, and he had to bend his head close to hers before he could hear the shame-faced murmur.

'Oh! Tony—you won't care for me any more now, because I'm half English!'

The ghost of a smile dawned in Anthony's tired eyes as he slipped his arm tenderly round her.

'Clare Castlemaine may be *half* English,' he whispered; 'but Mrs Anthony Farrell will be Irish—*every bit!*'

• • •

Upstairs in her own little room, kneeling before the picture of the Sacred Heart, Mary Carmichael was pouring out her soul in prayer for those who 'died for Ireland'. Her grief was very great, her heart torn with suffering and pain, and yet above and over all her sorrow was a feeling of pride and glory in the thought of those gallant young lives laid down so gladly—oh! so gladly! 'for Ireland'. She thought of Easter Sunday morning when in all parts of the city they had approached the Altar rails in their hundreds to receive the Holy Communion which was to be the Viaticum for so many of them—knowing the risk they were taking and realising that *they* would probably never see another Sabbath dawn over their beloved city. And yet willing—ah! and eager!—to light that spark which was to rouse their countrymen from their lethargy.

Weep not for them with useless tears;
but think of them with pride,
For Ireland they have fought the fight,
for her with joy they died.
We'll remember, we'll remember,
their blood, their wounds, their pains,
Tho' we know no pang was wasted,
not one drop was shed in vain!
For our country has awakened,
we have heard the trumpet blast,
The dream of slaves is shattered,
and we shall be free at last!
Lo! the dead arise triumphant,
and the living's task is set,
The cause is burning in our heart—
and we shall not forget!

CHAPTER XVII

FAITH OF OUR FATHERS

God's goodness has been great to thee!
Let never day or night unhallowed pass
But still remember what the Lord hath done.

Mary Blake was leaning back in a basket chair, in the garden of their house in Rathmines. There was a lilac tree in bloom this lovely evening in early June, and a hedge of veronica which formed the boundary between them and the garden next door was scattering its beauty and scent around. The garden was just beginning to look really well—wall-flowers, stocks, geraniums, pansies and carnations were all trying to bloom as gaily as possible.

The tears rose to Mary's eyes as she looked. It was the fist day that she had been out of doors for some time, as after the double tragedy in the family she had been prostrate for some weeks, and unable for any of her ordinary occupations.

Miss Jane Blake had come over from Rathfarnham to take control of her brother's house until Mary should be strong again, and it was well that they had her capable brain and hands to help them at this crisis.

Mary was very pale and thin, with a look of deep suffering in her kind eyes—those motherly eyes which had always looked so kindly on the young brothers and sisters for whom she had so tenderly cared. There were threads of silver in her hair too—and lines on the gentle countenance which had not been there a month ago.

Her gaze wandered over the garden now—sadly and wistfully. '*His* pansies!' she whispered to herself, 'and there are his prize carnations, and that scarlet rambler—I remember so well the day he first planted it. Ah! Shamus! Shamus!' Footsteps on the gravel walk made her turn her head, hastily brushing aside the tears as she did so.

'Oh! Anthony!' she cried out at sight of the visitor, 'is it you back again? And how is Mary and Clare?'

'I'm glad to see you are better, Mary,' replied Anthony as he seated himself on a garden chair beside her; 'it's good to see you about again—even if you *are* only a ghost of your old self!'

Mary smiled faintly.

'Yes—I'm much stronger, thank God!' she said; 'but tell me about the others, Tony, I'm so anxious to hear!'

And so he told her all about his visit south, and gave her all the loving messages with which he had been entrusted by both Clare and the other Mary.

'And when is the wedding to be?' she asked.

'In September, please God,' he answered. 'Clare did not want to leave Mary before Angel was able to go down to her, so we arranged for September, as by that time I suppose she will be able for the journey?'

'Oh, yes, I hope so,' said Mary, 'she is getting on nicely and will be able to sit up in a few days. I suppose' she added wistfully, 'there is no chance of Mary coming back to us?'

'No chance at all, I'm afraid,' he said; 'she never even alluded to such a thing, and then, of course, I did not speak of it either; but Clare told me she is certain that Mary will never return to Dublin.'

Mary Blake sighed.

'Well! after a while I must only go down to Co. Clare and see her,' she said, adding quickly, 'Here is Father, Tony—how do you think he is looking?'

Anthony's heart misgave him as he looked at Mr Blake—he seemed to have suddenly become a very old man and all his former life and energy were vanished.

But he would not add to Mary's troubles, so he only said, 'We must give him time, Mary, and then you will see that he will pull himself together again.'

Anthony went upstairs later to see Angel. The pretty room was as dainty and neat as ever—the window box was gay with flowers, and the canary was singing his little heart out. Angel alone was changed. Ah! yes—it was a different Angel who extended two thin eager hands to her visitor—older and graver, the sweet childishness that used to be her greatest charm was gone entirely, and in its place was a grave womanly look. And yet she did not look altogether sad—it was rather as if she had passed through the storm which had left its mark upon her for ever—but that now she had at last reached calm waters again.

'Oh! Tony! Tony! how are they?' she cried with something of her old impulsiveness.

And sitting beside her bed, her hands in his, he told her all his news.

'Oh! Tony,' she whispered when he had finished and they had been silent for a short time, 'you will be so happy—both of you! I know it. Ah! how good God has been to Clare. Why? Tony—*why*? and to us and to Mary Carmichael——'

It was the first time he had ever heard Angel question the Divine will, and he looked at her in surprise, but even before he could speak, she whispered, 'Oh! God forgive me! God forgive me! What am I saying?'

But Anthony said softly, 'Ah! Angel, His ways are not our ways! still we know "that those whom the Lord loveth, He chasteneth!"'

• • •

Clare came up to Dublin and stayed with the Blakes for a few weeks before her wedding, and Pat took Angel down to the country, and left her with Mary Carmichael. She was to stay for some months, and then her sister Mary had promised to go down for a while. They were determined that Mary Carmichael should not be lonely if they could help it at all.

'And surely *some day* she will come back to us!' So they prayed and hoped.

Clare Castlemaine and Anthony Farrell went into Retreat for nine days before their wedding. They parted at the commencement of the Retreat, and did not meet again until they stood before the Altar of God to pronounce their solemn vows. For them marriage was indeed a sacrament.

It was a quiet wedding—taking place at seven o'clock Mass, one bright September morning—but as she and Anthony knelt side by side to receive their Lord, with hearts full of love and thanksgiving, it would have been hard indeed to find a happier couple in all the 'four walls of holy Ireland'.

'And you are content, dearest?' her husband asked Clare, on the evening of the same day, as they stood side by side watching the moon rise over Bray Head.

'Oh! so content, Tony!' she said softly, 'and so happy—now that I have entered into my Irish heritage!'

'*Deo Gratias*!' said Anthony, reverently.

• • •

On that same September evening Mary Carmichael and Angela Blake were also watching the moon rise—over the trees of the lonely wood opposite the cottage.

'I suppose Clare and Tony are happy now!' said Angel, smiling: 'the world forgetting—by the world forgot, sort of thing!'

Mary laughed.

'We did not forget them, anyhow!' she said. 'I hope they got our wire of congratulations all right.'

There was silence for a few moments, and then Angel said softly, laying her hands on Mary's.

'And you, Mary? Have you forgotten? Are you content?'

'Forgotten—no!' was the low reply, 'but I am trying to be content—trying—oh, Angel! but it's hard sometimes!—trying to say—"Welcome be the will of God!"'

'Amen!' said Angel.

And so we leave Mary Carmichael, and let us take farewell of her in a few lines written in memory of another disappointed heart:

'This to your memory—who of yore
In patience love's sweet burden bore
By old Killala's wind swept shore.
For no one ever loved in vain,
And stricken sheaves yield golden grain,
When Love is purified through pain.'

MORE MERCIER BESTSELLERS

The Walk of a Queen

Annie M. P. Smithson

In *The Walk of a Queen* the scene is set in Dublin during the War of Independence and it is a fascinating story of passion and intrigue which holds the reader's interest from start to finish.

The Weldons of Tibradden

Annie M. P. Smithson

The Weldons of Tibradden follows the fortunes of three generations of the Weldon family beginning in the 1870s and ending in 1935. It is a fascinating story of success, courage, love and betrayal.

The Marriage of Nurse Harding

Annie M. P. Smithson

The Marriage of Nurse Harding, a story of love, bigotry and heroism, is now reprinted for the benefit of new generations who did not have the opportunity to read it.